SECRETS
of
THE V
Devotions f

By Dr. Bruce Wilkinson
Adapted by Rob Suggs
Illustrated by Dan Brawner

www.tommynelson.com

A Division of Thomas Nelson, Inc.
www.ThomasNelson.com

SECRETS OF THE VINE™ DEVOTIONS FOR KIDS

Published in Nashville, Tennessee, by Tommy Nelson®,
A Division of Thomas Nelson, Inc.

Copyright © 2001 by Bruce Wilkinson

Unless otherwise indicated, Scripture quoted is from The Holy Bible,
New King James Version (NKJV) ©1982, 1984, 1990 by Thomas Nelson, Inc.

Other Scripture quotations are from the following sources:
The *International Children's Bible®, New Century Version®* (ICB),
copyright © 1986, 1988, 1999 by Tommy Nelson, a division of Thomas
Nelson, Inc., Nashville, Tennessee 37214. Used by permission.
The Holy Bible, New International Version® (NIV), copyright © 1973,
1978, 1984 by International Bible Society. Used by permission of
Zondervan Publishing House. All rights reserved.

Library of Congress Control Number:
2002021947

Printed in the United States of America
02 03 04 05 06 PHX 9 8 7 6 5 4 3 2 1

CONTENTS

INVITATION
Ready, Set . . . Grow!

I BET I ALREADY KNOW something about you. I can tell you what your relatives say when they come for a visit. You walk up to Aunt Bernadine or Uncle Alphonso and they say, "My, how you've grown!" Happens every time, doesn't it?

But what if Aunt Bernadine could see not just how tall you've grown, but other kinds of growth as well? What if she saw a huge crowd of people you had influenced in good ways? Or a long list of your impressive accomplishments at school?

My, how you're about to grow! Not just in the physical space you take up, but in your power to make the world a better place. If you read the pages of this book each day, and then you allow God to use them in your life, you will begin to do something Jesus called "bearing fruit." And you're going to like it—a lot!

As you read each day's devotional, think about your own life. At the end of each day, I've given you a page to do some of your own writing and get you thinking about how you can put some of these exciting ideas to work immediately. May the words of Jesus change you enough that even Aunt Bernadine and Uncle Alphonso can't miss it.

"I am the true vine, and My Father is the vinedresser. Every branch in Me that does not bear fruit He takes away; and every branch that bears fruit He prunes, that it may bear more fruit. I am the vine, you are the branches. He who abides in Me, and I in him, bears much fruit. . . . By this My Father is glorified, that you bear much fruit. . . . I chose you and appointed you that you should go and bear fruit."
(John 15:1–2, 5, 8, 16 NKJV)

DAY 1
IT'S A DEAL!

*"I have obeyed my Father's commands, and I remain in his love.
In the same way, if you obey my commands, you will remain in my love.
I have told you these things so that you can have the same joy I have.
I want your joy to be the fullest joy."*
JOHN 15:10–11 ICB

DO YOU LIKE GRAPES? I hope so—you're going to be hearing a lot about them in the next few weeks!

It just so happens that Jesus had a lot to say about grapes during His last days on earth. He was talking to His best friends, and of course, He had a lot more in mind than fruit. When He spoke of grapes—planting them, tending them, and so on—He was really talking about you, me, and how God uses us. Grapes and vines were almost like "code words" for Jesus and His disciples, and that's why I like to call His incredible ideas the *Secrets of the Vine.*

Got it? Great. That's why I'm changing the subject to peaches!

No kidding. I'm not trying to make your head swim. It just so happens that I come from a part of the world where most of our baskets are filled with peaches instead of grapes. One day my family moved to a house way out in the country, and my neighbor had a famous peach orchard. He liked to say his fruits were "big as melons, sweet as nectar." That made my mouth water, and I decided to check it out.

You can imagine my surprise when I went to see these amazing fruits and saw nothing but trees leaning on sticks. Not a peach was in sight, only trees propped up by poles.

My neighbor explained the mystery for me. He told me to come back in a few months (this was early spring). He explained that it takes a little patience, but it's well worth the wait. So I took his advice and came back in midsummer. Well, there they were: great, juicy peaches. And then I could see what the poles were doing: They were adding support for the bulging crop of peaches on every branch. The branches would have snapped without them, and we'd have been wading in peach juice!

I'm Quite a Handful!

The air smelled wonderful as I walked through the orchard. I found myself talking to God. "I want my life to be like this," I prayed. "These trees produce bundles of delicious fruit, and I want to produce good things for You, too. I want to produce good friendships, good deeds, a good family, and more! I hope the angels have to

What the Bible says . . .
"I want your joy to be the fullest joy."

come and prop me up with poles! Lord, do what it takes to make my life fruitful, just as my neighbor worked to make his trees fruitful."

That little prayer pretty much sums it up—everything I want us to talk about over the next few days. What kind of fruit am I talking about? It's not grocery store fruit that you could top your morning cereal with—I mean those good things that grow out of our lives. I often meet kids who are doing amazing things for God. Jesus would say their deeds are their fruit, and these kids are growing a *handful*. Wouldn't you like to be a handful? Well, you know what I mean.

But here comes the hard part: You have to give something to get something. For example, my friend Tony makes a trade. He mows lawns in his neighborhood, and he gets spending money for his efforts. Those yards look terrific when he finishes, but he has to trade sweat, long hours, and he has to take care of his mower. Tony thinks it's a good deal. "I trade time and work for spending money and the cool feeling of seeing all those nicely mowed lawns," he says.

My neighbor trades his time and work for peaches. Tony trades for spending money and a feeling of doing something worthwhile. What will you trade your time and talents for?

Let's Make a Deal

Jesus has a great suggestion. He says your life can produce fruit, and the results will be so wonderful that you wouldn't even *believe* it if you knew all the details now. Your life's fruit can be sweeter than the best peaches—or grapes, for that matter. It can be more valuable by far than a little extra pocket money. It's better in every way than anything else you could trade your time and talents for. Are you feeling curious? Want to know the secrets?

Well, that would be telling! But I do plan on telling you. As my neighbor might say, "Come back in a few pages! It takes patience, but it's well worth the wait." Hey, that's another trade—a few minutes' reading time each day for secrets you can really use. I hope you'll read one of these chapters each day, maybe with someone in your family or with a friend. At the end of each chapter, I'll give you some special "Talk Back" chances to get you thinking and working on what you've learned.

Does that sound like a good deal? Let's shake on it—and see what fruits tumble out!

daY 1

TALK BACK

The best trade I ever made was:

One really cool thing I hope to get out of reading these chapters is:

WHAT'S THE BIG IDEA?

Great fruit springs from a tiny seed.
Great adventure springs from books we read.

DAY 2
THE BIG PICTURE

"I am the true vine, and My Father is the vinedresser. . . .
I am the vine, you are the branches."
JOHN 15:1, 5 NKJV

OKAY, HERE'S THE PICTURE.

Soccer is your game, and you're pretty good at it. Your team has the best record in town. You've spent countless hours practicing your sport, and you could hang in there with any team in the state. There's no reason you couldn't end up in the national tournament! That would mean a trip to the big city.

Your coach has called a special team meeting. Surely Coach will reveal plans for the play-offs and the national tournament! You and your teammates can scarcely contain your excitement. But the meeting takes a turn no one expected. Coach takes you out to a garden and starts to talk about—well, things that have nothing at all to do with soccer. Coach talks about setting a good example at school, about doing good things in the community. You sneak a surprised look at your friends. Why this? Why now?

That's how Jesus' disciples felt when they heard about the secrets of the vine. Ever since they'd begun to follow Jesus, they'd been thinking *big* thoughts about what Jesus and the team could do. After all, people in all the towns were talking about Jesus. The team might just go to the big city, Jerusalem, and take over the country! This could be *huge*.

Then, just as everyone had gotten all psyched for the awesome things that might happen, Jesus called a team meeting to talk about . . . *grapes*.

Grapes. Vines. Branches. The disciples probably sat there scratching their heads. Jesus wasn't on His way to sit on a throne in Jerusalem after all. He was about to be arrested and executed as a criminal. But the group didn't know this. All they knew was that He was comparing them to fruit!

GARDEN PARTY

Imagine you're there with Jesus in the garden, feeling the cool evening breeze. Think about how His words might have sounded to you. Here's what He said:

> "I am the true vine, and My Father is the vinedresser. Every branch in Me that does not bear fruit He takes away; and every branch that bears fruit He prunes, that it may bear more fruit. . . . I am the vine, you are the branches. He who abides in Me, and I in him, bears much fruit; for without Me you can do nothing. . . . By this My Father is glorified, that you bear much fruit; so you will be My disciples." (John 15:1–2, 5, 8 NKJV)

Just a few words, but they're powerful words—words that will change your whole life. Yes, we'll have plenty to talk about over the next few weeks. For example, think of these comparisons:

The vine is like Jesus. A vine brings sap (food) from the roots to the branches. Jesus' words nourish us.

The branches are like you and me. When we follow Jesus, we grow from being connected to Him, just like the branch grows from the vine.

The vinedresser is like God. The vinedresser gives careful attention to every single branch in a vineyard, helping each to bear fruit. God cares for you in that same way.

The fruit is like your good work in life. Get the picture? Just as a vinedresser tends the vine and its branches to produce delicious fruit, God gives you the strength through Jesus to do good things.

There's a lot there to chew on, isn't there? Fruit for thought! Of all the things Jesus taught His group of friends, He saved the most amazing for last. Before this time, the disciples only thought of themselves as people who followed Jesus. Now they discovered they were connected so deeply that even when He left, He would still be a part of them.

PIECES OF THE PUZZLE

Today we'll look at the big picture. Let's assemble the pieces of the puzzle:

- ☉ *The vineyard is all about what God has planned for you.* Jesus put each of us in this world to bear fruit.
- ☉ *The vineyard shows that God will tend to your needs.* Like a vine-dresser, He gives you plenty of care. He prepares you for all the good works ahead.
- ☉ *The vineyard shows that God will work with you all the time.* That means every day. Tending a vineyard is full-time work!
- ☉ *The vineyard shows that you're in this world to be a friend of Jesus.* A vine gives its life completely to the branches. That's just how closely you're connected to Him.
- ☉ *The vineyard shows that God wants you to know exactly what He is doing in your life.* Some people think God is mysterious and that we can't know Him very well. But that's not how it is with friends, is it?

So there it is—the whole picture. Take some time today to think about all that it means for your life. Use the Talk Back page to get you going.

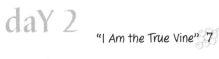

daY 2

TALK BACK

The most interesting thing I learned about God today was:

Being so closely connected to Jesus is a very big idea. Here is one way it will make my life different:

WHAT'S THE BIG IDEA?

The main activity in vineyards is growth. You're going to be doing a whole lot of that from now on.

DAY 3
IT'S NOT AUTOMATIC

And let our people also learn to maintain good works,
to meet urgent needs, that they may not be unfruitful.

TITUS 3:14 NKJV

I'VE GOT TO TELL YOU about what happened to Kimberly.

She comes from a musical family. Her mom and dad had met many years earlier, when they both sang in the same vocal group. After they got married and Kimberly came along, everybody said, "Your girl will definitely be a singer. How could she *not* be, with parents like you?"

Every time baby Kimberly cried, people said, "Listen to those pipes! A future rock star." Even today, when she calls someone to the phone, her mom says, "Don't strain your singing voice, dear."

Well, last week Kimberly finally looked into the whole singing thing. She decided to try out for the school chorus. A few grownups gathered by the doorway when Kimberly's turn came up. They knew hers was a musical family, and they wanted to see what this girl could do.

The piano player sat down at the keyboard, played a simple scale, and asked Kimberly to sing the notes. But when Kimberly opened her mouth and tried the first note, she sounded like a sick crow! Then she tried the second note. That one came out sounding something like a squeaky porch door. She surprised everyone.

Don't worry, Kimberly took it well. "Hey, so much for all that *natural ability*," she laughed as she turned to leave.

"Not so fast," said Mrs. Burns, the music teacher. "Your voice is fine—you've just never applied it to music before. You can have all the talent in the world, but the human voice doesn't tend toward music naturally. You have to train it. Becoming a fine singer doesn't happen all by itself. Join us in the chorus, Kimberly, and we'll have some fun developing your voice."

Makes sense, doesn't it? We all have *potential*, or what we might accomplish. We have to work to make that potential become *actual*. There aren't many great prizes you can win just by showing up. It takes a little work to be great at anything that really matters.

WANDERING AND WONDERING

Kimberly's story reminds me of grapes—okay, you knew that was coming!

I've found out a number of interesting things about vineyards. One is that they don't naturally produce great clusters of fruit. You'd think that with nature in charge, it would be sort of automatic—just leave the vines alone and wait for the awesome, abundant grapes.

But it doesn't work that way at all. Leave the grapevine on its own and you'll have one disorganized grapevine—sort of like study hall when the teacher leaves the room. The vine wanders all over the area. It twists here, twines there, and wraps itself around the nearest tree. You know what kind of grapes wild vines make? Small ones; bitter ones.

Those really big, sweet grapes your local grocery store carries didn't grow wild. They took some work. They were grown by wise, skilled vinedressers—people who have worked most of their lives to learn how to grow the best, most delicious, and most abundant grapes possible.

It's just like Kimberly's voice, when you think of it. Without training, her voice might sound like a crow with the flu. But with some work and some help from Mrs. Burns, Kimberly could become a songbird.

It's also like the fruit God wants to produce from your life. You won't produce an abundance of good works for Him naturally, will you? No, you'll have to work at it. You'll have to discover what kinds of good things you can do best. You'll have to work on becoming the kind of person who will do them. And you'll have to get started, growing in an intelligent way under the guidance of God and the people who love you. Otherwise, you'll be like a wild grapevine—wandering, wondering, skittering, and scattering in all the wrong directions.

KNOWING AND GROWING

I know you want to be all that God desires of you. You're not out to produce skimpy wild grapes. You'd rather create the best fruit around. The main point today is you can't make that happen just by showing up. You'll need to have the right attitude and do the right things at the right times. But don't worry; God will help you. Maybe that's why you've started reading this book and why you've continued to think about it these last three days. See? God has already begun to work, and you've already grown! You're in a much better position to produce good fruit than you were a couple of days ago.

Let's think about the seeds God has planted in your life. He has given you everything you need to grow into a remarkable person, today—a person who serves God fruitfully every day. What are your best talents? What are the best aspects of your personality? These are some of the seeds that can grow. How do you think God will use them?

It's exciting when you think about it. God loves you so much that He is already—*right this moment*—preparing you to do wonderful things for Him. Every day we'll draw another step closer. You were born with natural talent!

daY 3

TALK BACK

Some things take a lot of work. Here is something I've had to work on—but I'm getting better:

One thing about me that God must like, and that He's likely to use, is:

WHAT'S THE BIG IDEA?

Coal isn't very attractive or valuable. But if you apply the right kind of pressure for the right amount of time, you end up with a diamond!

DAY 4

MORE THAN A GAME

For we are His workmanship, created in Christ Jesus for good works,
which God prepared beforehand that we should walk in them.

EPHESIANS 2:10 NKJV

THE GAME BOX—that's Juan's thing. It's a little plastic container with four buttons that brings infinite amounts of fun.

When Juan touches the switch and the little "On" light glows, the games begin. Juan may carry out a mission, capture a monster, or grab three blocks of the same color in a row. The Game Box offers him hours of entertainment, and Juan wonders what kind of a genius could have possibly invented it.

Certainly, that kid he sees in the mirror couldn't have—not in thirty-seven quadrillion and a half years. Juan makes a nasty scowl at himself. He might as well; certain kids at school make fun of that face. They don't like his nose or his ears. However he combs his hair, they find fault with it. And when they pinch him, Juan can't even defend himself—not with these pencil-thin arms and this skinny frame.

When Juan looks into the mirror, he dislikes everything he sees. Then he turns back to his Game Box and captures a few more monsters.

"If only real life were as simple as one of these games," he tells his big brother, Fernando. Then the whole thing comes out. He tells Fernando about the kid in the mirror, the kids at school, the whole mess.

Fernando listens quietly, then says, "Juan, take another look

daY 4

in the mirror, Bro." Juan does just that, a little puzzled, as his brother picks up a Bible and reads a verse. It's the verse for today, Ephesians 2:10.

THE WORKS BOX

Juan has never thought about this before: He, Juan, is God's creation! The fellow who designed the Game Box has to be one smart dude, but how many more smarts does God have? *Infinite amounts*, that's for sure. But instead of designing computer consoles, God made elephants. And mountains. And stars. And *Juan*. Now that's one pretty wild thought—strange but true, to hear Fernando tell it.

If the smart computer guy designed the Game Box to play good games, then God designed Juan to do good works. According to Fernando, that means Juan's pencil-thin arms and skinny frame don't matter. Eyes, ears, nose—the whole "Juan console"—are exactly the way God wanted them to be.

> What matters is how God sees him.

The thing about the Game Box is that it's completely useless if you try to play games made by another software company. Juan tried it one time, and he got a blank screen. But if you play the right games on it, the exact ones written for the Game Box, you're in for some great times.

Hey, just call Juan the "Works Box"! As long as he finds the good works God made him to perform—not those God created someone else to perform—then Juan is in business. He'll do those things, and he'll do them really well. When you come right down to it, it really doesn't matter what Juan sees when he looks in the mirror. What matters is how God sees him. And God says, "Juan, you're better than an elephant;

trust Me on this. You're better than a mountain, and I made some *tall* ones. Stars? You're going to shine brighter by far. Just wait and see. It's going to happen when you get busy doing the things I have planned for you."

Juan takes one more look in that mirror. This time he takes a deep breath and watches his chest expand. He's not so puny after all. These arms—they'll do. They'll carry whatever load God designed them to carry. And what's that on his face? Something new—a smile!

GETTING TO THE GOOD STUFF

I want you to really think about today's reading, Ephesians 2:10. Consider this:

You are God's workmanship. Now, that's not a free pass to take it easy. It doesn't mean you can do something wrong and say God made you that way. But it does mean that your basic materials are fantastic! You are a first-class, grade-A product.

God created you for good works. That's your purpose. This is why you don't have that free pass to do wrong things. God has very definite ideas for you, and nothing else can make you as happy as doing those things well.

God made you to be focused and successful. He wants you to stay "on task" with the good stuff and to produce plenty of it. Quality matters, but so does quantity. Be sure to log in tomorrow for more on that one.

I can't think of better news that I could bring you. God loves you, He made you exactly the way you are, and He has really big plans for you. As soon as you and those plans connect, everyone will smile—you, God, and all the people around you.

Everyone grins, everyone wins! That's a deal better than you'll find anywhere—even on the Game Box.

daY 4

TALK BACK

Sometimes I think less of myself because:

But here is what God says to me:

WHAT'S THE BIG IDEA?

Next time you're feeling down, look up!
Somebody up there likes you.

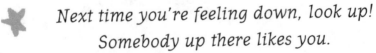

DAY 5
THE MORE THE MERRIER

"By this My Father is glorified, that you bear much fruit;
so you will be My disciples."

JOHN 15:8 NKJV

HAVE YOU EVER KNOWN two friends who loved each other a lot—yet competed at everything? My friends Valerie and Chin Li were like that. If Chin Li made an A in math, then Valerie had to have one. If Valerie got that new type of shoe, then Chin Li had to have a pair. There weren't many arguments between them; they just liked being equal!

Then they joined Girl Scouts—together, of course. Both of them did well on every single project. But you know what's coming, don't you? Cookies: boxes and boxes of cookies.

The Scouts were asked to sell cookies to help pay for their uniforms, supplies, and special trips. But there were some extra incentives. Selling a certain number of boxes earned you a T-shirt (big whoop!). A few more boxes got you a Game Box (a little better). Eventually, you could actually earn a new bike or a cool stereo system. (Wow!)

Chin Li and Valerie soon became cookie-selling fanatics. Their parents helped a little; aunts, uncles, and cousins bought a few boxes. But the girls discovered that the only way to get the really big sales was to go out and work the neighborhoods, house by house. They endured slammed doors and tired feet, of course, but their sales totals increased. Chin Li had her heart set on that bicycle; Valerie wanted the stereo.

daY 5

THE REAL PRIZE

But something sad happened. Chin Li went out to sell cookies in the rain, determined to reach her goal, and she got the flu. She had to spend the final two weekends of sales laid up in bed. There was no way she could earn any of the really good prizes. Her body was ailing, but her spirit sank even lower.

He is pleased when we give unselfishly.

Weeks later, the Scouts had their awards ceremony. Chin Li had gotten over the flu, but she couldn't get too excited about the ceremony. She hadn't wanted to earn the bike for herself; she wanted to give it to her dad. He worked two miles away and had to walk each way every day. Chin Li had wanted to earn a boys' bike and brighten his day a little, so he wouldn't always be so tired. The flu had ruined her dream.

At least she could be happy for Valerie, who led the troop in sales. She'd sold more than five hundred boxes. Chin Li expected to see a big stereo presented to her. But to her surprise, the troop leader rolled out an excellent blue bicycle. But Valerie already *had* a bike—why hadn't she chosen the stereo?

"Stereos are cool," Valerie said as they walked home, "but I knew your dad needed a bike more than I needed music. Anyway, I wouldn't have won anything if you hadn't talked me into joining the Scouts. And I'd never have sold so many boxes if I hadn't been so determined to beat your total!"

They had a good laugh over that one. And you know what? I have to think the Lord was laughing right along with them—laughing for joy. He is pleased when we give unselfishly. He's also pleased when we do our best and get good results. The key word is *much*, as in John 15:8: ". . . that you bear *much* fruit."

Fair Is Fair

Quality. Quantity. Which is most important? Why not give God *both*? He certainly deserves our best quality, *and* plenty of it. Valerie and Chin Li discovered they could be fruitful in selling boxes of cookies to help their troop. Once they got going, they discovered it was fun to be productive. By doing their very best, they also honored God in a meaningful way. After all, when Jesus talked about fruit-bearing in John 15, He set out four levels:

- *No fruit.* "Every branch in Me that does not bear fruit" (verse 2).
- *Fruit.* "Every branch that bears fruit" (verse 2).
- *More fruit.* "That it may bear more fruit" (verse 2).
- *Much fruit.* "That you bear much fruit" (verse 8; see also verse 5).

Sometimes we hear people say, "All that matters is that you do your best." But wouldn't you say that results matter, too? If I have brain surgery, I don't want the doctor to merely do his or her best— I want results! The Scouts could have given the same prizes to everyone, but they offered better rewards for better results. The truth is that if you really, truly do your best, you'll get those results.

Imagine Jesus watching as you, I, and all our friends bring baskets of fruit that we've worked hard to grow. Some bring empty baskets, others bring small ones, and some bring heaping baskets. Then you and your hard-working friends bring baskets spilling over with luscious fruit. Which baskets most please Jesus? It's a no-brainer.

Think today about how you can do *much more* for Jesus. What would most please Him? What is the fruit of the day? When you think of it, God will be pleased—and I predict that you will, too.

daY 5

TALK BACK

I think that God cares about results because:

Here's one way I can produce good results that will please God today:

WHAT'S THE BIG IDEA?

Great effort brings great results, and great results bring great rewards. Go for the top!

DAY 6
WATCH OUT FOR WORMS!

Dear friends, you are like visitors and strangers in this world . . . People who do not believe are living all around you. They might say that you are doing wrong. So live good lives. Then they will see the good things you do, and they will give glory to God on the day when Christ comes again.

1 PETER 2:11–12 ICB

JUSTIN COULDN'T GET TOO EXCITED about his new church at first. His mom and dad pointed out how exciting it could be to help start a new one. They said to focus on creating a new place to help people get to know Jesus.

Justin missed his old church, where many of his best buddies attended. This new one met in a school gym just to get started, and only two or three kids Justin's age came. That's why he decided to start inviting some friends to the new place.

But many of his friends already belonged to churches. His parents said that the best way to build a new church was to invite nonbelievers who didn't attend anywhere—then they would begin bearing fruit of the very best kind. They could help people come to know Jesus for the first time.

Justin saw the wisdom in that. He thought about Shane, who played on his basketball team but didn't have a church. Justin jogged up to his friend after practice and asked, "What are you doing this weekend? Some of us are starting a new church, and it'll be a lot cooler if you're there. Wanna come?"

Shane's reaction surprised Justin. His friend just stared back at

daY 6

him for a moment, then turned and left. *What was that all about?* Justin wondered.

The next day Justin caught up with Shane during a water break. "Are you mad at me or something?" he asked.

"Not really," said Shane. "It just seemed weird—you asking me to church. Isn't church all about 'do unto others' and stuff?"

"Sure, that's part of it," said Justin. "What's your point?"

"Well, remember last week, when we were tied with the Blazers, near the end of the game? You told me how you tripped their center under the basket to keep him from getting the ball."

Shamed, Justin looked down. Shane's observation hit him like a ton of bricks.

"You were kind of proud of that," Shane continued, "so I just wondered what kind of church you went to, that's all."

Vineyards Are Outdoors

Here comes one of the tough parts about this whole fruit business. Being fruitful for God isn't something you do all by yourself, free of outside interference. In one way, it's everyone's business.

Think about where orchards and vineyards grow—outdoors. Fruit needs access to the sun, the rain, and plenty of fresh air. You're growing your fruit out in the open, too—where people can see. God's kind of fruit always has to do with people, because He cares more about them than anything else. He loves His children, and He wants us to love them by serving them. As you work on figuring out how He wants you to bear fruit, this will be your first clue: It will probably have something to do with helping others.

Justin did exactly the right thing by inviting a friend to church. But he discovered a worm had gotten loose in his orchard: He had done something that was wrong. No one expects Justin to be perfect, but he has to realize that people are watching all the time. If he calls himself a Christian, those people will expect him to behave in a way they can admire.

No More Worms

Let's look at our Scripture verses for the day. Peter wrote that we should watch how we behave because there are people around us all the time who don't know much about God. They do know that God's people supposedly do the right thing. But if they see us behave poorly, they receive the wrong message. It may look like our faith doesn't make any difference in the way we live—that our standards of conduct are no better than anyone else's.

But Peter also says that the good things we do make a big difference. When people see our good works, they will begin giving the credit to God. Hey, that's a pretty exciting thought!

What the Bible says...

So **live good lives.**

I hope you don't get the wrong idea. I hope you don't think that as soon as you make a mistake or a poor decision, you can't ever bear fruit for God again. Wow, that couldn't be more wrong. The Bible is filled with stories of people who messed up, then went on to do great things for God. God never gives up on us, and He always offers us a fresh start.

The most important thing to remember is that your fruit tree is planted right out there in public. Anyone can walk up and inspect the baskets of fruit you're producing for God. Much of that fruit will be about loving and serving those people. But watch out for worms! They say one bad apple can spoil the whole barrel.

Look over the fruit of your life today. The Talk Back section will help you make sure your fruit is healthy and delicious.

day 6

TALK BACK

I need to set a good example for those who are watching me. Here's one situation where I know I should be particularly careful:

I know that God will always help me bear good fruit. Here's my prayer asking Him to do that in my life:

WHAT'S THE BIG IDEA?

We have to grow fruit outdoors—but outdoors is a messy place! Take good care of what you're growing.

DAY 7
LAND OF THE GIANTS

"Eye has not seen, nor ear heard,
Nor have entered into the heart of man
The things which God has prepared for those who love Him."
1 CORINTHIANS 2:9 NKJV

IMAGINE VISITING A LAND WHERE giants walk the earth. You can feel the thundering footsteps on the ground beneath your feet. Boom, boom! You can see the trees being pushed aside as these massive giants take their giant steps.

Suddenly, you realize what it feels like to be an ant or a grasshopper. Some lumbering giant could step on you without even realizing it! You certainly don't want to become a human pancake on the bottom of a giant's shoe. So you run for cover, just in time to miss being hit on the head by a big, juicy apple.

And I do mean big—this apple is almost your size! It stands to reason, doesn't it? Big people have big fruit.

Believe it or not, there's a story in the Bible that might remind you of the scene I've just described. It's all about the time when the Israelites were seeing their new homeland for the first time. Have you heard this one? You'll find it in Numbers 13. This was Canaan, the land God had promised, but the Israelites were a little nervous about going in and claiming it. Who knew what dangers lurked there? So Moses sent spies to check everything out, and they came back with some jumbo grapes: "[They] cut down a branch with one cluster of grapes; they carried it between two of them on a pole"

daY 7

(Numbers 13:23 NKJV). Just imagine a cluster of grapes that required two big, sturdy soldiers to carry it.

I've never seen such a thing in my grocery store—how about you? For that matter, I've never seen a giant-sized apple.

AGES AND STAGES

God had always promised the Israelites He had a wonderful land for them, a place where the fruit was abundant and delicious. In the same way, He promises a bright future for you and me. Only the grapes have changed.

The fruit we grow may not be the literal kind anymore. But God still helps us to grow wonderful things for Him. As I know you remember, we define our own fruit as anything that brings Him glory and makes Him happy. We've been talking about this kind of life for a week now, and it's time to begin thinking: Just what is the fruit in your life? What, exactly, is God working on in your life, so that you can be a fruitful believer and servant?

That's quite a question, isn't it? Perhaps a good way to think about it is to imagine Jesus walking into your room, smiling, and sitting down to talk with you. You and Jesus discuss all the exciting things going on in your life. You also talk about all the challenges and problems you'd like to overcome. Then He says your name gently and continues, "You and I are working on bearing fruit together, aren't we? Remember how you came to understand that I'm the vine, and you're one of My branches? Your life is going to produce wonderful fruit, and it's beginning to happen through . . ." How do you think He would finish that sentence?

It's important to remember that you're still a young branch. As your life goes on, God, the loving vinedresser, will make adjustments to help you move from one stage to the next in fruit-bearing: from *no fruit* to *some fruit* to *more fruit* to *much fruit*. Be patient. The important thing is to begin to see *where* He is working in your life.

FRUIT INSPECTION

Where, then, are the areas where you can make God look good? (That's another way of saying, "give God the glory.") Let me throw out a few:

- *Doing your schoolwork.*
- *Pleasing your parents.*
- *Joining clubs and teams.*
- *Being a good brother or sister.*
- *Being a good friend.*
- *Becoming active in church activities.*
- *Caring for possessions.*
- *Helping kids who need a hand.*
- *Developing your talents.*

Wow! That's quite a list, for starters, and I bet you could add several more items. What thoughts did you have as you looked at those areas of fruitfulness? Are there things you'd like to add? Where are your strengths? Where do you need some work? They're all important areas for pleasing God, but let's focus today on your strengths. In the list, circle the area where you're the strongest (add to the list if you'd like). Which item, when you read it, made you smile and say, "Hey, that one's going well for me!"?

Perhaps there's already a little fruit on your branch. Thank God for what He has already done to help you in those areas. It will only get better. Perhaps someday you'll need to call a friend and say, "Come give me a hand. This cluster of fruit is so huge, we have to build a shed for it in the backyard. It will take two of us just to carry it!"

I don't know about you, but I want to live in the Land of the

daY 7

Giants. I want to grow some of those gigantic grapes and amazing apples. Seeing that kind of fruit would put a big smile on my face. And I might even realize that, while I was busy growing fabulous fruit, I became a giant, too.

Talk Back

Here is where God is doing the most good in my life, and here's why I think that:

Here's a way that I can please God *even more* in that area during the next few days:

What's the Big Idea?

Today's sprout is tomorrow's full branch.
That's a heavy thought!

Day 8
SHAKE OFF THE DUST

My son, do not despise the chastening of the LORD,
Nor detest His correction;
For whom the LORD loves He corrects,
Just as a father the son in whom he delights.

PROVERBS 3:11–12 NKJV

MITCHELL AND TABITHA WERE EXCITED when they got their first jobs last summer. Their dad owned a small company that manufactured gaskets—paper-thin, circular pieces stamped out of metal and plastic. Eventually, the gaskets go inside engines, where they prevent leaks.

It was the kids' job to separate the gaskets from the strips of material they were cut from. Their dad felt they were a bit young, but he agreed to pay them for this task. He offered them a one-week trial to see how well they performed.

On their first day, Mitchell and Tabitha really came through. With thoughts of their earnings, they worked through box after box. They did almost as well on their second day. But by the third day, their fingertips were a bit red and sore and their minds were a bit restless. As Mitchell stood by the loading dock, taking a break, he realized the gasket in his hand would fly really well. He threw it, Frisbee-style, and watched it soar magnificently over several factory roofs.

Naturally, Tabitha had to give one a whirl. Before they knew it, they started competing to see who would earn the gold medal in the Long-Distance Gasket Fling. They sent a good number of them skyward.

Well, that contest came to an abrupt halt. A "labor neighbor" paid a call on Mitchell and Tabitha's dad, and he brought with him a large handful of gaskets and an angry expression. Dad was none too pleased about how his kids had spent their time. So much for their summer jobs! But I have a feeling Mitchell and Tabitha will do a little better next summer. They learned a tough lesson.

Sticking to It

Mitchell and Tabitha had a very clear responsibility: to fill boxes with gaskets by the end of each day. Jesus gives us a similar responsibility. He speaks of baskets rather than boxes, but the idea is the same: He wants us to have something to show for our time. Jesus actually told a number of stories in which "the Master" gave out assignments and then left. He returned later to see how His workers had done. It's clear that we have a wonderful friendship with Jesus, but we also have very definite responsibilities.

When He was talking about the vine and the branches, Jesus said something surprising. He said that He cuts off the branches that don't bear fruit (John 15:2). The first time I read that verse, it made me nervous! If I'm a branch, the last thing I want is to be cut off. But as I learned more about this whole grapevine business, I heard an interesting thing.

A vinedresser once told me about vines that don't bear fruit. Quite often, he said, branches will trail along the ground. Dust and mud get all over them, and that's not good for them. It stops the branches from bearing fruit. I asked the vinedresser, "What do you do with those branches?"

He replied, "We watch very carefully for those dusty, dirty ones. Then we lift them gently and clean them off. We tie them back into place, and soon they bear fruit just as they should."

LIFT ME UP!

But what about cutting them away? I went back and studied the original language (Greek) that recorded Jesus' words. Sometimes, you know, words can have different meanings when we translate them into a new language. The word that we have in the Bible as "cut off" actually has the very meaning that vinedresser described. The true meaning is "take away" or "lift up" rather than "cut off." It tells us just what a vinedresser does for ailing branches.

Boy, that's a lot better! It says several things to me. It says that if I go off in the wrong direction as Mitchell and Tabitha did, I trail in the dirt a little bit. I get a little dusty and don't bear the fruit God wants me to bear. In those times, I've found that the Lord lifts me up, cleans me off, and puts me right back to work. Then I can start bearing fruit again, just as He wants me to.

Are you a little **dusty**, a little **musty**, a little **rusty**?

Have you ever made some poor choices or simply stopped doing the things you should be doing? Maybe you disobeyed your parents somehow, or stopped working on your grades at school. It could be many different things. I'm sure it has happened in your life before, and it will happen again. Rest assured that you can be lifted up in those situations, if you'll simply ask Jesus to help you out. He will give you a fresh start and a new opportunity. Then, like Mitchell and Tabitha, you'll be an even better, more fruitful worker because you'll be a little bit wiser.

How about today? Are you a little dusty, a little musty, a little rusty? If you haven't done much to make God happy in the last few days, now is the time to talk to Him about it. He'll help you shake it off.

daY 8

TALK BACK

When I think about God, the kind vinedresser, lifting me up, here is how that makes me feel:

Here are some ways God will help clean me off and put me back to work when I take the wrong path:

WHAT'S THE BIG IDEA?

Dust is an amazing thing. It collects quickly, quietly, and almost invisibly. But it can cover almost anything. Ask God to help you keep the dust away.

Day 9
ATTITUDE ADJUSTMENT

"I am the LORD your God,
Who teaches you to profit,
Who leads you by the way you should go.
Oh, that you had heeded My commandments!
Then your peace would have been like a river,
And your righteousness like the waves of the sea."

ISAIAH 48:17–18 NKJV

WHEN I WAS GROWING UP, our family dinner table had a firm set of rules. They weren't posted on the wall or written on paper. I don't even remember them being stated out loud. But we kids understood. I'll tell you how they worked.

When we came to the dinner table, it was time to clean up our act. We were normal, rambunctious kids, but when dinnertime came, there were rules. It was as if a "No Nonsense" sign lit up on the kitchen wall. It was time to eat, chat, and behave.

But you know how it goes. Sometimes it was just too much to ask us to stay in line. Maybe my brother would pull a funny face when he knew only I would see. He knew exactly how to make me laugh uncontrollably. I would try to stifle myself, but a little snort might escape. I knew exactly what would happen next; it was in the unwritten rules. I would get *the Look.* That was the first warning, and it consisted of nothing more than a sharp glance from my father. Or he might conspicuously clear his throat: aa-*HEMMMM!*

This, of course, caused my brother to double his efforts to push me over the edge. He might kick me under the table. He could count on me to take the bait and retaliate—and we all know that he who retaliates gets caught. At that point, I would get the second level of warning: my name. Dad would give me *the Look* and sharply say, *"Bruce!"* At that point, I would have strong incentive to straighten up and fly right. Believe me, I had no desire to move on to the third level. We'd been there and done that. The third level wasn't a warning but a side trip. Dad would take me into the next room and make certain that the dinner table nonsense came to a rapid end.

> God **lifts** us up when we get **bogged** down and **stop** bearing fruit.

Only on rare occasions did any of us reach level three, and we never found out whether there was a fourth level. If I *had* found out, I might not be here to tell you the story!

It's All about Discipline

I'm sure you could tell a few stories about dinner table rules enforcement. But what does that have to do with vines, branches, and fruit? Actually, everything.

Yesterday we discovered the first secret of the vine: God lifts us up when we get bogged down and stop bearing fruit. Another word for that is *discipline.* But wait a minute—how could *lifting up* and *discipline* mean the same thing? One seems rather nice, the other harsh. But true discipline is about correcting misbehavior. God often does that by reaching into our lives, showing us where we've gone wrong, and getting us back on the right track. Parents, teachers, and coaches do this for us, too. We're not usually thrilled to receive correction, of course, but later we realize it was just what we needed.

Does God have his own version of dinnertime rules? Yes, He does. We often fail to recognize it when God gives us the equivalent of *the Look* or an *aa-HEM!* But He does it just the same. Perhaps He'll make you feel a tiny twinge of conscience. That is His gentlest way of calling attention to the fact that you're starting to get into the dust, as branches often do. The hand of God is so gentle upon your shoulder that you probably won't even recognize it as His.

If you persist in the wrong behavior, there will be a slightly louder "wake-up call"—the equivalent of *"Bruuuce!"* This will come in the form of *consequences* to your misbehavior. Perhaps you get into some trouble at home or school. You know that actions have consequences, but you might not have considered that sometimes God is speaking to you through them.

The third warning, of course, is the most difficult of all. We can cause a great deal of pain and unhappiness in our lives by ignoring His loving guidance.

Preventive Maintenance

Here comes the good part. At my dinner table we knew the rules, and most of the time we avoided the need for discipline. It's the same way with following God's plans in your life. Bearing fruit for Him is a great, rewarding pleasure. Who would rather trail in the dust than bear a load of beautiful grapes? Not me; not you. But just in case we go astray (and we will, of course), it's good to know in advance what the consequences will be. That helps inspire us to get back to the pleasures of fruit-bearing.

Have you gotten a wake-up call lately? The little twinge of conscience, perhaps, or some kind of punishment at home or school? It's great to know that being disciplined is entirely an option. Why not choose instead to get back to juicy, delicious fruit-bearing?

TALK BACK

It happens to me, too! Here's an example of "unwritten rules" in my home:

I can remember a time when God "lifted me up"—and I didn't even realize it then:

WHAT'S THE BIG IDEA?

God's discipline is gentle at first. You never need to find out about the more serious levels.

DAY 10
THAT LITTLE VOICE

"My son, do not despise the chastening of the LORD,
Nor be discouraged when you are rebuked by Him;
For whom the LORD loves He chastens,
And scourges every son whom He receives."
HEBREWS 12:5–6 NKJV

AHMAD DECIDED HIS NEW physical education teacher was cool in the extreme. He'd been a little nervous about coming to a new school. It helped to get an instructor who seemed . . . well, like a regular guy.

To start with, Mr. Shanks acted younger than most teachers. He let kids call him by his first name, Bob. He could make kids laugh, too. Bob looked out for Ahmad; he'd noticed Ahmad's case of nerves. He was as much a friend as a teacher.

During his second week at school, Ahmad felt a little more relaxed. He thought he'd try a little humor himself. He clowned around during calisthenics, getting into some crazy positions. The kids around him laughed. But Bob saw what Ahmad was doing, and he frowned. For a moment Ahmad felt embarrassed. Yet it also felt good to make people laugh, and two minutes later he demonstrated a ridiculous sit-up. Everyone laughed but Bob, who knelt beside him and said, "C'mon, Ahmad! Get it in gear, dude."

The rest of that period, Ahmad stayed in line. But the next day, he saw the other kids watching him during PE. His fans wanted him to perform; he couldn't let them down, could he? Finally,

Ahmad started fooling around again. He thought he could pull off a couple of stunts without getting caught, but his plan failed. Bob pulled him out of the group and sent him to run laps.

That was no fun at all. He'd thought Bob was his friend!

STRICTLY SPEAKING

At the end of the class, Ahmad found Bob waiting for him. The teacher patted Ahmad on the back and said, "Hey, I realize you're new and you're trying to make some new friends. That's cool, in its own time. I'm sorry you had to learn the hard way that this is *class* time—my time. And it's all about exercise and discipline, an important part of athletics. I can't just let you slide because you're new. Come to me anytime you need to talk. But during class time—*my* time—we'll use our hour *fruitfully*."

Okay, maybe he didn't actually use the word *fruitfully* there at the end. But it helps us make our point, doesn't it? This is all part of the secret that has to do with how God works when we take a wrong turn. Like that friendly but disciplined PE instructor, God looks out for us. He puts us in the right place and guides us in what He wants us to do for Him. But sometimes we foul up. God uses discipline to get us back on track simply because He loves us. He wants us to be happy in the long run, and we have important work to do.

"For **whom** the LORD loves He chastens . . ."

Ahmad found out about the "long run," didn't he? Yes, you probably recognized Bob's style. It followed yesterday's three stages of discipline from the dinner table. First Bob gave a stern look, next he called Ahmad's name, then he imposed some true punishment. Ahmad was hurt, but was wiser afterward. And he grew a tiny bit in his ability to be a first-class fruit-bearer.

Do you see that *discipline* is often another word for love? It's important to remember this when life becomes difficult. You might shake your fist at the sky and say, "God, why are You letting this happen to me?" That's fine. But afterward, remember to ask the real question: "Lord, what are You trying to teach me in all this?"

REBUKING, CHASTENING, SCOURGING

Hebrews 12:5–6 (NKJV) actually includes all three of those stages. The first is *rebuking*. "Do not . . . be discouraged when you are *rebuked* by Him" (v. 5). The second stage is *chastening*. "For whom the LORD loves He *chastens*" (v. 6). It's about the way we feel inside when we know we've continued to do wrong. We're upset. We're in turmoil.

Also in verse 6 is this idea: "He *scourges* every son whom He receives." *Scourging* is another word for punishing. This is all about genuine physical punishment. In Jesus' time, repeat offenders were whipped severely. It was called a scourging. Ahmad had to run some laps when he failed to obey his gym instructor.

What about you? Years from now, if you continue to ignore what God is gently trying to show you, if you move past the rebuking and chastening stages, you could face great punishment. God loves us and wants the very opposite for us. He'll do nearly anything to lift us out of that dust and see us happily bearing fruit. Discipline and punishment come only when we insist on willfully disobeying.

So the next time you hear that little voice, somewhere deep inside you, saying, "Hey, you know that's not the best choice," be encouraged! You're feeling God's gentle rebuke. It means He is right there by your side, helping you not to fail.

daY 10

Talk Back

I remember a time when a teacher taught me a lesson in a gentle way:

I can understand why God uses rebuking, chastening, and scourging. Here's what I think:

What's the Big Idea?

Life is one big class where we often learn our lessons the hard way. But the Teacher is cool in the extreme!

Day 11
Someday You'll Get It

For they indeed for a few days chastened us as seemed best to them,
but He for our profit, that we may be partakers of His holiness.
Now no chastening seems to be joyful for the present, but painful;
nevertheless, afterward it yields the peaceable fruit of righteousness
to those who have been trained by it.
HEBREWS 12:10–11 NKJV

HAVE YOU EVER BEEN ASKED to watch a young child, even for a few moments? I'm talking about, say, a two-year-old. If so, you know it's an adventure. There's a reason babysitters make good money!

Vanessa has a little brother about that age, and he isn't exactly the bundle of joy she expected. Oh, she loves Scooter. (Don't you love the nickname?) But she thought that having a baby brother would involve a lot of holding and hugging. Instead, ever since Scooter got his legs under him, it's been more about chasing and preventing. An hour of Scooter-duty leaves Vanessa feeling like she's just completed a skateboard marathon—and she was the skateboard.

Scooter's life mission is to hold, examine, then chew every object in the universe; Vanessa's mission is basically to stop it from happening. Life would be easy if she could just put Scooter in his playpen, but he needs to move around. So Vanessa takes care of him while Mom does the grocery shopping. She tries to keep him interested in his approved, teething-ready toys, but Scooter's gotten bored with them. He wants to handle knick-knacks on the coffee table. He wants to taste the fountain pen. He wants to get his chubby fingers on the glass ornament that has been in the family for a century.

Each time he grabs, Big Sister nabs. "No!" she says, intercepting his hand and placing the tempting object out of reach. To Scooter, it's an outrage. He can't find a corner of the room where she won't bound in and spoil his fun. After a while, he gets frustrated and pulls one of his best heavy-duty tantrums. Scooter pounds on the floor and screeches at the top of his lungs.

All Big Sister can do is wait for him to finish venting, then hug him and love him and tell him, "I know it's tough. Someday you'll get it. Someday you'll understand."

LOVE IS EXASPERATING

Sometimes I feel about God the way Scooter does about his sister. "Why can't You leave me alone, Lord? Why are You always grabbing my hand just as I'm about to get hold of something good? Why do You always spoil everything?" And I want to have a tantrum of my own. Don't worry; I don't roll on the floor and scream—not quite. But there are times when I want things my way, even though I understand that God knows what is best for me.

Scooter would like to stick his finger in the electric socket. He'd like to perch precariously on the table. He'd like to do any number of things that, from his perspective, seem like fun. A mature perspective sees them as terribly dangerous. Vanessa's protection seems mean and cruel to Scooter. Someday he may thank her for carefully guiding him away from the dangers he couldn't recognize.

There are many dangers you and I can't recognize. There's the danger of wrong decisions every day. There's the danger of hasty words that might wound someone we care about. There's the danger of missing out on the best, most satisfying things in life—the fruit God wants us to bear for Him. God doesn't discipline us because He's mean and cruel. He does it because He loves us so much that He'd rather listen to a tantrum or two than let us hurt ourselves. He doesn't want us to damage the beautiful futures He has set before us—if only we could see them.

I think that in those times, God smiles and says, "I know it's tough. Someday you'll get it. Someday you'll understand."

UNDERSTAND NOW!

This is exciting—it's one of the first milestones of true wisdom in your life. This is where you accept discipline as a *correction that had to come*— and you change your course. It's the time when you're hurting, when something has gone wrong. But still you say to God, "Thank you. I understand now where I went wrong, and I know you wanted something better for me. Thanks for helping me through discipline, even though it's painful."

What the Bible says...

No chastening seems to be joyful for the present.

Perhaps you've done something to hurt a friend. You said something mean behind her back, and she found out. Discipline is the trouble that has disrupted your friendship and the sorrow you feel about it. A friendship is one of those very places where God wants you to bear fruit. He wants you to bless other people, but it will be difficult for you to do that if you let them down. So you realize you've messed up, you talk with God about it, and you go to your friend and apologize. As a child, you thought saying you were sorry would immediately make everything better. But now you know it takes time. That's part of the discipline. You're going to have to work on that friendship and earn some trust again.

And you know what? You're going to be stronger and wiser for it. You'll trust God more. You'll be more focused on pleasing God. It's tough now, but someday you'll get it. You'll understand.

daY 11

TALK BACK

Hey, I'm no baby! I'm grown up. But in some ways, God watches over me like Vanessa watches over Scooter. Here's how:

When I realize that it takes time to understand what He is doing, I have these thoughts about God's care for me:

WHAT'S THE BIG IDEA?

Baby steps! That's how we learn the ways of God. Realizing that means you've taken one giant step.

Day 12
The Case of the Giant Candy Bar

Create in me a clean heart, O God,
And renew a steadfast spirit within me.
Psalm 51:10 NKJV

I WISH I STILL HAD a certain old comic strip to show you. It made me laugh, and it made me a little sad. There was a lot of truth packed into those funny little panel drawings.

In the first panel, a kid was at the pharmacy, studying the candy rack. There he saw his favorite candy bar, a Gooey Slab, in its bright red wrapper. His mouth watered as he thought about how good that Gooey Slab would taste, if only he had a dime. (This was a *really* old cartoon!)

The next thing we saw was the same kid walking out of the pharmacy. This time the little drops of moisture were no longer coming from his mouth—they were dripping down his forehead. By the way he held his coat closed, we realized he had taken the candy without paying. He looked from side to side for twenty police cars to come screeching up at any moment, sirens wailing. We could see the Gooey Slab sticking out of his pocket, miraculously bigger than it was in the store.

As he arrived home, the kid's mother called, "Is that you, Junior?" His eyes had bugged out. He answered, "Yes! It's just me! I didn't do anything!" Of course, she hadn't asked. But that candy bar was now the size of a loaf of bread. It just kept growing and growing.

Finally, the kid made it to his room, and the candy bar had gotten almost too big to stow in his closet. He just sat across the room from it, staring and thinking, *What am I going to do with this thing? I certainly can't eat it!*

UNFINISHED BUSINESS

The truest thing about that cartoon was the way the Gooey Slab kept getting bigger. There was no explanation, but I understood. In the boy's mind, it started out as a small thing. Why not help himself to a tiny little piece of candy? What was the big deal?

Yet after he took it, the crime kept growing and growing in his mind. His conscience had begun to work overtime. I like to think

What the Bible says . . .

Create in me a clean heart, O God.

God was working on him a little bit, too. As we've seen, He imposes discipline when we get off on the wrong path. Another word for "wrong path" is *sin*, and it has a way of growing and growing when it gets into our lives. We wonder how it could have ever seemed so small when we made our choice. But those sins grow until they block out every good thing God wants for us. In a way, they become "the boss of us." We can't get them out of our mind, and it gets much tougher to hear God's voice. We know something has gone terribly wrong in our friendship, and we need to make it right.

One day I sat on a hill in Oregon and asked God to show me all the "Gooey Slabs" in my life. I hadn't stolen anything, but I knew there were sins that were getting between us—some of them I wasn't even aware of. I got out a pad of paper and just began writing as

God helped me remember them. You could almost draw a cartoon of me making that list, and it would be funny and sad, too, because that list kept growing and growing. I had some sins to deal with—couldn't believe how many!

After that, I got on the phone and called people I had hurt in some way, even in little ways. I made some moves to make things right in cases where I had taken the wrong path. And I spent a lot of time talking to God, seeking His forgiveness and promising to do better. Of course, I knew my sins were already forgiven. That's the great thing about serving Jesus.

A Clean Getaway

I wonder what might show up on your list today. Have you ever stopped to think about what actions and attitudes might be keeping you from becoming all that God wants you to be? Remember how we discovered that the vinekeeper cleans off the dusty branches to help them start bearing fruit again? The dirt weighs them down until they're stuck in the mud. Maybe it's about time you got under the hose!

It feels really good to confess these things to God. The Bible tells us He forgives us completely and joyfully. You'll feel like a great load has been lifted from your back. You can start by praying what King David did, in the verse at the top of today's reading. He wrote that psalm after he had made a terrible choice that completely disrupted his life. But he came clean with God and went on to bear tremendous fruit.

Ask God to create a clean heart in you, and to help you make a clean getaway from those "Gooey Slabs" that weigh you down. Those sins, unconfessed, will become such a heavy load that you'll never take the journey God has mapped out for you. But come clean daily and you'll be amazed by how rewarding your journey will be.

daY 12

TALK BACK

That candy bar story reminded me of something I once did:

Here is one thing I want to talk with God about. I know He'll help me make it right:

WHAT'S THE BIG IDEA?

Nothing is as soothing as a good warm bath—and nothing makes you clean like the kind God gives.

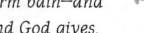

Day 13
Lions and Tigers and Bears, Oh My!

*Being sorry in the way God wants makes a person change
his heart and life. This leads to salvation.*

2 Corinthians 7:10 icb

Dorothy, the Scarecrow, the Tin Man, and the Cowardly Lion make their way through the darkest part of the forest. Remember that scene? It's from the movie *The Wizard of Oz*, of course, and it's one of those parts of the movie that really frightened you when you were a little kid.

Dorothy and her friends come to a sign that says, "haunted forest." Under that, the sign adds, "witch's castle 1 mile." This frightens the little group, but the next sign along the road gets more personal. It reads, "i'd turn back if i were you." The Cowardly Lion almost faints when he reads that one.

In an entertaining story like *The Wizard of Oz*, we're glad Dorothy and her friends ignore the signs, because we like action. But real life works a little differently, doesn't it? If you're hiking and you see a sign that says, "no trespassing," you know you're likely to get into trouble if you keep heading where you're not supposed to go. If you see a sign that says, "beware of dogs," well, you've been warned. Proceed at your own risk. As Dorothy says, "Lions and tigers and bears, oh my!"

You'll find that life is like a journey with important signs along the way. Some of them aren't printed clearly on a piece of plywood, but they're signs just the same. Those are the ones we've been talking about this week: little messages that are God's way of saying, "NO TRESPASSING." Keep going and the signs might become a bit more personal: "I'D TURN BACK IF I WERE YOU!" And if you're really stubborn enough to ignore the warnings, you may end up somewhere you didn't intend at all. You may find yourself lost or trapped, thinking, *There's no place like home.*

CAN'T YOU READ THE SIGNS?

The Bible has no cowardly lions, though there were some non-biting ones that Daniel encountered. But you'll find plenty of stories about God sending signs to the people He loved. "TURN BACK! CHANGE YOUR WAYS! DANGEROUS CURVE AHEAD!"

God often sent His signs through human billboards called *prophets.* These men and women often brought messages the people didn't want to hear. "If you don't turn back to God," they said, "and if you don't get out of the dirt and start bearing fruit again, you're going to bring about your own destruction." If you'd like to read a good example of that kind of message, check out the story of King Asa and the prophet, Hanani, in 2 Chronicles 16. Asa was David's great-great-grandson, but he began to tune God out. He started listening to advice that was not great-great at all! When Hanani came to him and pointed this out, the king didn't want to hear it. He threw the prophet in prison.

After Asa ignored the sign of the prophet's words, the signs became more personal. He was sick all the time, and he didn't know why. Even when he became seriously ill and close to death, he refused to pray for God's help. If only he'd known how to read the signs!

Of course, there are also stories of good sign readers—people like King Josiah in 2 Kings 22. He led his entire nation out of the darkness of their bad behavior and back toward God. We call this *repentance,* which means a complete turnaround in behavior. It means leaving the old ways behind forever—and deciding to follow God's way.

VINEYARD: NEXT EXIT

Today is a day to think about the signs in your life. Are you good at finding them?

What at school do you need to turn around? How about in your family life? Are there signs that something isn't the way it should be—for instance, do you have trouble getting along with a brother or a sister? If you find yourself getting into regular arguments, that's a bad sign. If you're taking good care of your duties around the house, that's a good sign. As you can see, there are a lot of areas and opportunities for taking either the right path or the one that leads into the dark forest. It's important to know the signs, isn't it?

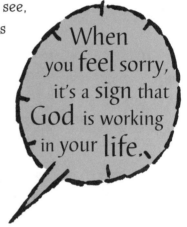

When you feel sorry, it's a sign that God is working in your life.

When you discover an area where things aren't right, you'll feel bad about it. Bad sign? Nope—a good one! Read the beginning of today's Scripture selection: "Being sorry in the way God wants makes a person change his heart and life" (2 Corinthians 7:10 ICB). Did you know that when you feel sorry, it's a sign that God is working in your life? That's His gentle hand on your shoulder and His voice saying, "C'mon, this is something you and I can work on and improve. There's no fruit ahead on that path. But if you get back on the road I showed you, you'll appreciate the results! Just follow Me."

That's when you stop feeling sorry and make your turn. After a while you'll wonder how you ever got off the path. It's true: There's no place like home.

TALK BACK

Here are some signs—both good ones and not-so-good ones—that I can see in my life right now:

Here's how I can make the turnaround and go back to God's way of doing things:

WHAT'S THE BIG IDEA?

Everyone takes a wrong turn every now and then.
It's good to have a Guide to show us the way back.

DAY 14
SHAKE IT OFF!

Then Jesus said to them, "Children, have you any food?" They answered Him, "No." And He said to them, "Cast the net on the right side of the boat, and you will find some." So they cast, and now they were not able to draw it in because of the multitude of fish.

JOHN 21:5–6 NKJV

"WOW, PETER, YOU'VE DONE IT this time!"

I can just see you and me following Simon Peter down the road, through the villages, and toward the shore. We like Peter—we really do—but we feel the need to brace him for what's coming. "He loved you, Peter. Before He came along, you were just another guy casting for fish. But He made you someone who casts for souls. You failed Him."

We see the pain in Peter's eyes. We know he's heading back to the place where life was simpler—back where he could cast for fish. We gently say, "He tried to warn you, Peter. Jesus said you'd deny Him three times before the rooster crowed, yet still you told those people that Jesus was not your friend. You know the discipline is coming."

With the next cry of a rooster, Peter has been fishing all night with his friends, catching nothing and caring little. He's too deep in his thoughts to notice the stranger who asks how the fish are jumping. *Not at all; nothing seems right anymore.* The stranger says something about breakfast, and asks the men to drop their nets one more time. For some reason, they do just that and get a boatload of fish! That's when they gasp as they realize the stranger's name.

daY 14

Over breakfast, we listen with surprise as the risen Jesus takes Peter off to the side. But we don't hear harsh words. We don't hear, "You blew it, Peter, and it's going to cost you." Instead we hear the kindness of a good friend—not even a mention of Peter's disgrace. "Do you love me?" Jesus asks. When Peter replies that he does, Jesus says, "Feed my sheep."

We realize Peter has already been disciplined through the terrible feeling he's had to carry within himself. And now, Jesus is lifting him gently from the dust, saying, "Bear fruit for me."

LOVE LIFTED ME

So Peter "got off light." What a week it's been! It's challenging enough to learn so much about God's discipline, but just when we thought we had all the answers—someone changed all the questions!

That, my friend, is the constant surprise of life with Jesus. Yes, it's true that He disciplines us. It's true that when we fall, He'll lift us up and point us back in the right direction. It's true that correction can be very painful. But we can't ever lose sight of the fact that beneath all this discipline lies *perfect love.* Our limited minds could never understand how deep and wide that love is. Try to imagine the highest number there is or the boundary line where the universe ends. You can't do it. God's love is like that—infinite. And because it's so awesome, it keeps taking us by surprise. We're always shocked by how strongly we *feel* that love after we've failed.

I think that's how Peter felt when Jesus came to him and patched things up. There was no need to talk about the past. God never emphasizes how far we fell yesterday, but rather how high we can jump tomorrow. "If you love Me," He said to Peter, "forget about yesterday and go love other people." You're going to find that bearing fruit always comes down to that—loving others.

Can we really get that idea into our heads? When God says

we're forgiven, He means it! He's not going to dwell on what went wrong, and He doesn't want us to do so, either. Hey, harvest time is coming. There's too much work to be done to sit around and mope.

PETER, PETER, PEOPLE FEEDER

This week I've encouraged you to think about the places in your life where you may have stumbled in the dirt. I've tried to help you get acquainted with the stages by which God disciplines us. But I've never asked you to pitch a tent and camp out in the muck of what went wrong. That's just another kind of dirt that chokes out the fruit, isn't it?

God loves you yesterday, today, forever, inside-out, from your head to your toes.

For Peter, discipline was that terrible period between the morning he denied Jesus and the morning Jesus told him to shake it off and get back to work. Peter's story after that proves he became a world-class fruit-bearer. As a matter of fact, this very man who failed so miserably became the church's first great leader. Since God had completely forgiven him, what a terrible waste it would have been if he'd never forgiven himself. But he did, and he brought in quite a harvest. He fed the sheep—God's people—just as Jesus wanted him to.

God loves you yesterday, today, forever, inside-out, from your head to your toes. You love Him, too, but you'll never be so perfect in the love you give back. He knows that. Just remember that when you stumble, you'll find out just how deep His love goes. And that will make you eager to climb back up, shake off the dust, and do great things for Him.

daY 14

TALK BACK

I've never really taken in just how much God loves me. Here's how I used to think of His love:

Knowing He'll never hold my failures against me makes me feel this way:

WHAT'S THE BIG IDEA?

When the past is in your sights, it's out of place.
Put it back behind you where it belongs.

DAY 15
ALL THE TRIMMINGS

*"My Father is the vinedresser. Every branch in Me
that does not bear fruit He takes away."*
JOHN 15:1–2 NKJV

YOU'VE JUST MOVED WITH YOUR FAMILY to California, right to the heart of the wine country. You decide you'll take a shot at this whole grapevine thing, and your new California friends help you choose all the stuff you'll need—grape stock, trellis, everything. So you do the planting, the watering, and then the hard part: waiting! But you're surprised just how quickly the growth comes. There's the vine, then here come the branches. Boy, you'll be eating a big bowl of juicy grapes in no time. Look how full and lush that vine is!

There's only one problem. Time passes, and no rich, sweet grapes appear. All you get are puny, bitter grapes. You tell your friends how disappointed you are. "Hey, spare us the sour grapes," your friends say. Then, after the bad joke, they take pity on you and show you the secret you missed. It's called pruning.

"Pruning?" you ask with raised eyebrows. "I'm not into prunes. I thought we were going for grapes." Your friends roll their eyes and agree that one bad joke deserves another. Um . . . that *was* a joke, wasn't it? Then they see you lack a gardening vocabulary, and they begin to explain as their shears *snip, snip, snip* to illustrate their points.

Pruning doesn't mean growing prunes. It means cutting away excess growth. They explain to you a principle of good gardening.

There's nothing more—well—*enthusiastic* than a branch springing to life. It sends out extra growths, extra offshoots, and it blooms out in every direction. That's wild growth, but we're interested in the best grapes possible. By pruning, we cut away the extra vines that take away sun and sap from the grapes.

A few snips of the shears and the pruning is done. Soon your vines produce juicy grapes, and you experience "shear" happiness! That's a groaner, and your friends tell you to "cut it out"—though they don't want to be "snippy." (Enough!)

A GRAPE, GRAPE JOY

Please don't stop reading! I promise to prune away the bad jokes. I don't want to choke out the incredible truth we'll be learning this week. This one is so useful, so eye-opening, that it's going to make you see your whole life in a different way. I bet you'll start putting it to use as soon as you finish reading.

> Have you **ever** felt "maxed out"?

This one is all about the activities and interests that fill the basket of your life. I bet you lead a busy one. Have you ever felt "maxed out"? Maybe there was a time when you found yourself hurrying from school to Scouts, from Scouts to team practice, then home to take a bath and do your homework—then you fell asleep, only to wake up and start all over again? At some point you may have realized you weren't going to survive like that. You couldn't do everything and be everywhere. You had to decide what was most important, then drop the least important activities. Mom told you that dropping school was *not* an option, so perhaps you snipped out Scouting or some other activity. Whether you realized it or not, when you dropped something, you were pruning your life. The most important things in life need your time and focus—otherwise they'll languish on the vine like bitter grapes.

Our second secret of the vine is that the moment you begin bearing fruit, God will reach into your life and prune it. He will cut away anything that keeps your fruit from being plentiful and spectacular. That's what we'll explore during the next few days. How does God prune us? What do those heavenly shears feel like? Does it hurt?

Read on.

On God's Cutting Room Floor

What's your favorite movie? I can guarantee you that, when the director was filming it, he or she did some pruning. Most directors film lots of scenes, then watch all the footage in what they call the "cutting room." In the end, they trim away any scenes that detract from the story. They may have been good scenes. The director may have hated cutting them out. But doing so brought focus to the film.

Your life needs focus, too. Jesus said that He placed us here to bear fruit, and to bear much of it. In the movie that is your life, you'll probably find some "extra footage"—things that take away from the story God wants to tell through your actions. Can you be a good film editor and cut the extra stuff out?

The first thing you'll think of is activities—some club, hobby, or computer game that devours a little too much time. It could be certain friendships that work against your bearing fruit for God. It could be the simple "busyness" that snares most of us at some time or other. That's what I want you to begin thinking about today. God wants you to focus on the things that really count. He'll give you the wisdom to know where to apply the shears. It makes all the difference between the sour and the sweet.

TALK BACK

The busiest time of my life was:

I believe the most important part of my life right now is:

 # WHAT'S THE BIG IDEA?

*If you're doing much more and enjoying
it much less—you need a trim.*

DAY 16
LASER-EYE FOCUS

Turn away my eyes from looking at worthless things,
And revive me in Your way.
Establish Your word to Your servant,
Who is devoted to fearing You.

PSALM 119:37–38 NKJV

CHRISTOPHER IS ONE OF THOSE born athletes. I've known plenty of kids like him, both boys and girls. You can work hard and be a good athlete, but some are just born. Christopher has excelled at team sports since his first year of tee-ball.

As soon as he was old enough, Christopher was signed up for Little League baseball, Pop Warner football, school soccer, and church basketball. And given his blazing speed, he was looking forward to track and field when he got to high school. But last year something happened he never expected. Football league registration was just a week away when the doorbell rang one night after dinner. It was Coach Jenkins, whose team Christopher had played on the previous year. Had he worked out a way to get Christopher on his roster again? That would be *awesome*.

But Coach Jenkins had almost the opposite suggestion. He was there to urge Christopher *not* to play football this year! What was up with that?

"I knew I'd take you by surprise," said Coach Jenkins with a smile. "You're a great kid and a great quarterback, and I'd love to coach you again. But let me throw out an observation. Your football potential is pretty good, but your basketball potential is a slam dunk! I saw you when our churches played each other last winter. You're a natural. I don't say this to many kids, but I think you could end up with a college scholarship somewhere if you keep improving your game. But serious basketball is a twelve-month sport. You need to go to the summer camps and the clinics. You'll start high school before you know it. Now's the time to perfect your hook shot."

Christopher and his dad thought it over. They decided Coach Jenkins was right. Even though it was hard to sit in the stands and watch his buddies play football, Christopher figured a sacrifice now could pay off in a big way down the road.

THE BETTER FROM THE BEST

I think Christopher made a very wise and slightly painful decision. Think of his God-given athletic ability as "sap" (No jokes! That was yesterday). Christopher could have channeled that energy in any of several directions, to several sports. He could have a great time

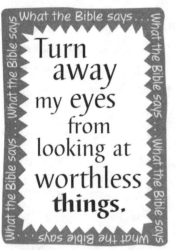

on various fields and courts year-round. That would be good—but would it be best? If his goal is to have a great time all through the year, it would be. But if his goal is to gain a scholarship for college education, perhaps it wouldn't. A trusted family friend believes he can bear better fruit if he *focuses* his production.

I can't think of a better example of pruning (if I could, you'd have just read it). What makes pruning so difficult for us is that sometimes we're not choosing between the good and the bad—we're choosing between the good and the better, the better and the best. I must tell you that I have a lot of fun doing many different things in my life. It's been very, very difficult for me to cut away the least important activities lately. As I prepared to teach a Bible study group this very idea, I wrote the following sentence in the margin of my notes: "I've discovered that I'm more a lover of leaves than a farmer of fruit." What does that sentence mean to you?

Pruning often involves cutting away things we don't want to give up. A grapevine is really beautiful when it grows wild. If we were going for the greenery, we'd simply let it go. But we've decided we want good grapes, and plenty of them. So we'll see that all the sap possible is focused on those grapes.

Beam Me Up!

Many of us have lives like a 40-watt light bulb. It has a nice, pleasant glow that it sends in every direction. It provides enough light for the room. But God wants us to have lives like laser light. Have you ever thought about the laser that plays your music CD or your DVD movie? It casts its light in a way that is extremely intense, highly focused, and pure in frequency. The result is incredible power, and it accomplishes scientific feats of all kinds—from reading your computer CD-ROM to performing surgery at the local hospital. I think God wants us to have "laser eyes" when it comes to fruit-bearing. As we discover what we do really well, and what will bear the most fruit for God, we turn it up to high beam and burn! Laser fruit—now there's a concept.

I wonder what's in store for our friend Christopher. I think it's entirely likely that his hook shot will earn him tuition at a fine college. And from there, even if the National Basketball Association doesn't work out, he can use his college diploma to do even more for God. By that time he'll know a lot more about fruitfulness. He'll discover that working with God is even better than a game-winning three-point shot from midcourt at the buzzer. You can't lose.

TALK BACK

Have I taken on too many activities? Here's what I think:

Here's what I dream of doing for God if I had laser-eye focus:

WHAT'S THE BIG IDEA?

Be the magnifying glass for God to shine through.
You'll set the world on fire.

Day 17
The Good Doctor

The works of His hands are verity and justice;
All His precepts are sure.

PSALM 111:7 NKJV

WHITNEY WENT INTO THE HOSPITAL last summer. She needed heart surgery—serious stuff. There was quite a prayer chain going during the week leading up to the surgery. All her friends from church and school lifted her up throughout the day and night. During that week before the surgery, Whitney herself talked to God more than she ever had.

It all started with a routine checkup by her doctor that revealed an irregular heartbeat. The doctor didn't like the sound of it, and he arranged some tests. Weeks later it was confirmed: Her heart had some minor problems that needed attention. For the time being, she was in no danger. Down the road, as she grew up, those problems might have become more serious.

The heart specialists recommended surgery. They explained the whole procedure to her clearly with charts and pictures of happy people who'd had the operation in the past. Everything would be fine. Whitney was very nervous, of course, but in the end, one factor gave her courage: the confidence she saw in her doctor's eyes. She knew she could trust her heart to him.

As the date for Whitney's heart surgery grew near, she found that God gave her new strength. So did the prayers of her friends and family. She could *feel* them all praying for her those last few days. And I'm delighted to tell you that the operation went smoothly—mission accomplished. Whitney had trusted a team of doctors to perform the most delicate of surgeries on her heart, and she came out stronger. Now Whitney loves life in a brand-new way. She takes up everything with new enthusiasm, and she serves God with all her strength.

You know what? I don't think the doctors were the only ones who worked on Whitney's heart. I think God did some surgery of His own.

FATHER KNOWS BEST

Can you remember a time when you really had to trust someone? Maybe you loaned your friend ten dollars. Maybe you depended upon a brother or sister to keep a secret. Maybe, as a very small child, you jumped from the side of the pool into a parent's waiting arms. Each time, you trusted someone.

All His precepts are sure.

What the Bible says...

Whitney looked into the doctor's eyes and knew he would take care of her. She also knew that God was with her. Heart surgery in the operating room is very scary. But there's another kind of delicate work on the heart that God performs. He is constantly operating on His children—cutting things away, making other things stronger.

When you were younger, perhaps you had a childish tantrum or two. I'm sure that's far behind you now. Why? It's been cut away, along with lots of other childish behavior.

As you grow older, you keep on cutting and cleaning up your act. Did you know Paul wrote about that? He said, "When I was a child, I spoke as a child, I understood as a child, I thought as a child; but when I became a man, I put away childish things" (1 Corinthians 13:11). We all stop them, but it doesn't happen all at once. That's the tough part. Life is a continual process of putting away childish things. We learn new, more grown-up ways to talk, to think, and to make plans. Everyone does that, but those who are particularly wise—and who really love God—trust His loving, gentle hand to keep on cutting. It's the only way to bear the fruit we're capable of bearing for Him.

Sometimes it's a little frightening. At those times, we ask our friends to remember us in prayer. We do a lot of our own praying. And we look into the heavenly Surgeon's eyes and know He can be trusted.

It's All about Trust

So where are you with all this? As you think about your life today, is God trying to tell you something? As you've read these last few entries, has there been some nagging thought about something in your life that needs to be pruned? (That's another word for surgery, of course.)

Stop and think. If God wants to make you wiser and stronger (and He does), this is a prime time for Him to make His move, isn't it? You're reading a book about bearing fruit. You're thinking some big thoughts about your life—maybe some of the biggest and most mature thoughts you've ever had on the subject. Those are just the conditions God wants for a breakthrough. He's got you right where He wants you!

That's why I want you to read today's verse a couple of times. Know that "everything he does is good and fair," and that means *everything*. Know that He can be trusted, completely. If He is calling you to take a step forward in your friendship with Him, let it happen. Let Him do the surgery and cut something out of your life that doesn't need to be there.

It's frightening at first—it's exhilarating and exciting in the end. Just ask Whitney.

TALK BACK

Does God want me to cut something out of my life today? Here's what I think:

Here are the reasons I trust God with everything in my life:

WHAT'S THE BIG IDEA?

The heavenly Surgeon can be trusted. He has infinite experience, and He's never lost a patient.

DAY 18
PRUNING FOR BEGINNERS

The LORD will perfect that which concerns me;
Your mercy, O LORD, endures forever;
Do not forsake the works of Your hands.

PSALM 138:8 NKJV

I HAVE A FEELING YOU'RE going to like this one!

You're at home, listening to some tunes on your portable stereo. There's a loud knock—everyone knows you have your headphones on. When you open the door, it's your brother or sister, who says, "This guy is here to see you. He came in a long, black car, and there are Secret Service agents with him! All I know is that he's from Washington, D.C., and he's some kind of special adviser to the president."

As you make your way to the living room, you also find out that he took a close look at your brothers and sisters and seemed disappointed. But now, as you walk into the room, the man begins to smile. "This is the one," he says. "The next president of the United States."

Your family begins to laugh; everyone thinks it's a joke. "The Oval Office will never be clean again," says your mother. But this important-looking government official is completely serious. He whisks you away in his limousine, and soon you're on a plane heading for the nation's capital. You're taken to the current president, who likes to borrow your portable stereo (it seems to help his stress).

So far, so good. But things turn sour when the president begins to get jealous. You've become quite the media favorite, with your face constantly on television and magazine covers. Soon your best buddy, the president's kid, tells you there's a conspiracy against you! After that, you spend years moving around the country, trying not to be assassinated.

Pretty wild story, huh? If you turned this one in at school, your teacher might send you to the nurse for a checkup. But actually I've just retold a Bible story, modernized the backdrop, and placed you in the starring role. It's the story of David, King Saul, and a whole lot of pruning. You can read the whole story beginning in 1 Samuel 16.

THE VALLEY THAT LEADS TO THE MOUNTAIN PEAK

Imagine how you'd feel if you, like David, were preselected to rule a great nation. You might think you'd arrived on Easy Street. But David had to pass through miles of trials to finally get to the good part. There were years of hiding in caves, running for his life, and wondering if God had forgotten him.

The same thing happened to all the great fruit-bearers in the Bible, and it will happen to you. God gives us the promise, but then a great deal of pruning and character-building must follow before we can become all that God has planned us to be. Let's look at some basic ideas about pruning:

- ◉ It's not a punishment. It happens because we're doing right, trying to serve God.
- ◉ It's not something we do. God does it to help us.
- ◉ It's difficult to recognize at first. It's all mixed in with everyday life and relationships.
- ◉ It can be confusing and frustrating, but it develops our abilities and aptitudes that delight us.

How successful it turns out depends on how much we cooperate with God.

Imagine yourself as the president tomorrow. How good a job

would you do? No offense, but I don't think you'd be ready! You know how it works: no pain, no gain. If you want to make good grades at school, you have to study. If you want to become a good musician, you have to practice. If you want to become a good athlete, you have to train. That's life.

With God, it's a little trickier because we don't always recognize His pruning when it comes. But after the fact, we can often say, "It was You all the time, wasn't it, Lord? Now I get it—thanks!"

It's All Good

If I could have you take away one "aha!" thought from today, and really nail it down in your life, it would be this: The tough times, when we're really struggling to grow up a little bit more, *don't* mean God is angry with us. They mean He cares enough to work on us. You're a branch on the verge of producing extraordinary fruit. Feed yourself on the dreams of the big things you can do for God—the abundant fruit you'll soon bear. Remember that, right now, God is delighted with you. We tend to think He's the most pleased when all is calm, and every hair is in place. Not so! God is most pleased when you come up against some kind of wall, struggle with it, and break through to something better.

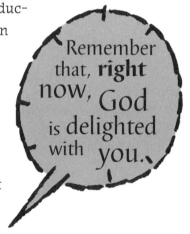

Remember that, **right** now, God is delighted with you.

He's proud of you. He's preparing you. And don't ever forget that He's present for you, too. Ask Him to bless you and give you the strength you need. He's going to answer that prayer every time.

I have no idea whether you're going through "presidential pruning," but I can tell you this: Whatever He has prepared for you, it's good. It's *all* good!

TALK BACK

There was a time when I wish I'd realized it was God working on me. That time was:

Just for fun, I'm going to imagine what I could do for God someday. Here goes:

WHAT'S THE BIG IDEA?

You have to cross the valley to get to the mountain.
But the view from the top is fantastic!

Day 19
The Joy of Misery

My brethren, count it all joy when you fall into various trials, knowing that the testing of your faith produces patience. But let patience have its perfect work, that you may be perfect and complete, lacking nothing.
James 1:2–4 NKJV

REBEKAH GOT A HEAD START on dreading the seventh grade. She began dreading it all the way back in third, when her brother gave her a blow-by-blow description of all his miseries. She tried to remember that grade seven was four whole years away. That might as well be forty years to a third grader.

Still, her fear of seventh-grade tortures always sat in the back of her mind. And suddenly, it happened. She was twelve and a member of Mrs. Graham's seventh-grade class. This was the year when math became officially impossible. This was the year when you had to write long reports with all kinds of impossible requirements. This was the year of icky science experiments and having to climb the rope in physical education. *No way* Rebekah was going to survive seventh grade.

You're expecting me to say it turned out great? Sorry, but it was pretty much as hard as she expected. Naturally, Mrs. Graham was known to be the toughest teacher in the school—in the universe, according to some accounts. On the first day of school, Mrs. G warned the kids to expect a tough year. "And I'm not going to make it easy on you," she said. "If you're struggling with your math, let me know. We'll schedule some tutorials. If you can't write an essay paper, well, we'll work on it. But I'm going to expect the best work from you, and you can expect the best teaching from me. Regardless of what you've heard, not a single student has ever died while doing my homework."

Rebekah had to laugh at that joke, which broke the tension a little bit. By midterm, she had a few Cs, and some of them were trying to dip even lower. She gritted it out, started to catch on, and the funniest thing—near Christmas, she realized she actually liked Mrs. G, toughness and all. Rebekah was learning to be a student.

DON'T WORRY, BE HAPPY

Our Scripture verse for today seems bizarre the first time you look at it. It tells us you can expect to have all kinds of trouble, and when the trouble comes—be happy! *You've got to be kidding,* we think. *First you tell us it's going to hurt. Then you tell us to be sure and smile while it's hurting. Get real!*

But read the rest of the passage. It tells us *why* we can be happy about bad times:

- God is testing our faith.
- Testing our faith teaches us patience.
- Patience helps us on the road to perfection.

What was that last word? *Perfection?* This just gets stranger and stranger. But God defines perfection as that place where He has us just where He wants us: bearing fruit and being exactly what He designed us to be. Then we're complete, lacking in nothing.

Rebekah will never be the *perfect* student. She's simply not made like those whiz-kid prodigies who go off to college at age twelve. But she's on her way to something much better: perfection at being what God wants her to be. Part of that is learning to work very hard, learning to handle the pressure of tough tasks, and learning not to become frustrated and give up (that's called patience). Mrs. Graham is helping her in that whole process. As a matter of fact, God is using Mrs. Graham in Rebekah's life more than the teacher will ever realize.

Sometimes all of that comes together in your mind. Like Rebekah, you suddenly step back and take a good look at yourself. *Wow!* you think. *I may not be there yet, but I've come a long way. No way could I do a math word problem like this back in September.* And the best part about it has nothing to do with math. The best part is that you've learned patience and that great results are worth waiting for.

I LAUGH IN THE FACE OF DANGER!

Let's face it—tough times are tough times. Nobody ever said they'd be easy. But when you've come to the place where you can see

them for what they are, and have a good laugh right in the middle of it, you've really shown some maturity. Step to the side, wait until nobody's looking, and give yourself some applause!

Count it all joy when you fall into various trials.

Many of your friends will be discouraged. Some of them won't understand why they're struggling in school, or having problems with their friends, or just having tough times. But you have the gift we call *perspective.* You see that God is doing something. Perhaps you can watch out for your friends and help them get that same perspective. Encourage them. Tell them God isn't through with them yet. Help them see that crossing the finish line makes it all worthwhile.

That's what true friends do. It's just another stage in becoming a true bearer of delicious, plentiful fruit. You'll help others bear fruit, too.

TALK BACK

It helps to know why life is hard sometimes. Here's how that makes me feel about God:

Here's the name of a friend who is having some hard times right now—and how I can help:

WHAT'S THE BIG IDEA?

When the going gets tough, the tough get perspective—and a big grin.

DAY 20
I WANT WHAT YOU WANT

"But seek first the kingdom of God and His righteousness, and all these things shall be added to you."

MATTHEW 6:33 NKJV

LAST YEAR, JIM DECIDED TO pray that he'd become the best student in the class.

He already made good grades, but he knew three girls and one guy who always out-achieved him. If he made a 90 on the social studies test, they'd all get grades between 91 and 100. Jim was tired of coming in fifth—he wanted to be the *best*. So he prayed for that every morning.

Jim did a little better that semester. He found he was more focused and eager to attack his books. But he never became better than the third best student in the class. That bothered him. Why hadn't God given him what he prayed for? He decided to ask Mr. Simpkins, his Sunday school teacher, for help.

It was odd. When Mr. Simpkins heard that Jim was praying to be the best student, he said, "Good!" But when Jim explained why, Mr. Simpkins didn't say *that* was good. Instead he kept smiling and asked a question: "Jim, are you certain you want what God wants—and for the same reasons?"

Jim had never thought about that before. Wanting to be a better student was good. But Jim's reason for wanting that had to do with beating other kids. Maybe a *better* motive—the kind God might share—would be to become a smarter, more disciplined person who is prepared to serve God even better. Jim hadn't exactly prayed it that way.

Mr. Simpkins said, "The key to prayer, Jim, is not only to want what God wants, but also to want it for the right reasons. Let's try an experiment. Think about how God might use you in your class. That's something you can always be sure He wants. If you want it, too, ask Him for it."

> Go for what God wants, and **many** other things come with the deal.

Jim thought about that for a few days, and this became his prayer: "Lord, help me continue to do my best, and show me how I can serve You today among my friends." Jim couldn't believe how that prayer changed things. Suddenly, he found opportunities to help other kids with their homework. He even became better friends with the students who were out-achieving him.

And you know what? Those kids gave him some good pointers. He's on his way to being the best student in the class—for all the right reasons.

SEEING THROUGH GOD'S EYES

When Jim prayed his first prayer, God was listening. Jim became a better student, but mostly because God helped him focus more on schoolwork. But when Jim prayed the second prayer, he hit God's bull's-eye. He made a Matthew 6:33 prayer (that's today's verse). He decided to get on the same page with God—to try wanting the same things He wants. That's the kind of prayer that will immediately change your life and mine, because God is just waiting for us to ask.

The funny thing about it is that it *doesn't* mean wanting a whole bunch of boring stuff. The things God wants are the same things we'd want if we were smart enough to want them! For example, Jim discovered that being used by God among his friends was exactly what he'd always desired; he just hadn't really thought about it directly. The first time he asked, he prayed it sincerely, but more from his mind. Now he prays it every day, and he prays it with all his *heart*. He loves it when God uses him to make someone else's life better.

Make that verse, Matthew 6:33, the theme of your life this week. And please don't miss the back end of the verse, which says something pretty exciting: Go for what God wants, and many other things come with the deal. That's why Jim is on his way to becoming the best student now.

RIGHT REASONS, RIGHT RESULTS

Guess what? Seeking what God wants is just another way of pruning. We cut away the things that are not what God can use. We're preparing to bear fruit, just as Jim is bearing fruit at school now. As you say the "pruning prayer" (*Lord, I want to be used by You. I only want what You want.*), you will notice the following changes in your life:

- ◉ You'll begin to use your *time* differently.
- ◉ You'll begin to use your *talents* differently.
- ◉ You'll begin to use your *treasures* differently.

If you think about it, that pretty much covers all that you possess. There isn't a thing you have that God can't use. And all of it will become better and more pleasing when you hand it over to God. When you ask for the right reasons, you'll begin to see the right results.

Have you asked God to help you want the things that He wants? Today happens to be an excellent time to make Matthew 6:33 your prayer. Good timing, huh?

daY 20

TALK BACK

As I read Matthew 6:33, here is what it means to me:

Here is what I think God wants for me within my circle of friends:

WHAT'S THE BIG IDEA?

Tell God what you want, ask Him what He wants,
and soon you'll find they're the same thing.

DAY 21
TRAVEL LIGHT

But one thing I do, forgetting those things which are behind and reaching forward to those things which are ahead, I press toward the goal for the prize of the upward call of God in Christ Jesus.

PHILIPPIANS 3:13–14 NKJV

JEREMY MADE HIS FIRST SKI trip last year. He couldn't wait to get on the road with his church group. He'd always looked forward to skiing for the first time. He still looks forward to it.

His first mistake was letting Mom pack for him. She was worried about whether he'd have enough sweaters; perhaps he'd need an extra blanket. By the time Mom had finished, Jeremy had two bulging, heavy suitcases.

He found out just *how* heavy while carrying them across the parking lot to the bus. He didn't want to look weak, so he carried both suitcases *plus* a third one. He had generously offered to carry Sharon's little suitcase, which barely fit under his left arm. That was his second mistake. Then, of course, he had the huge box of cookies his mother had baked for the trip. He cushioned it under his right arm. Then there was the extra jacket he might need later in the day; he clamped it down with his chin.

Every step was murder; he felt like the Iron Giant. Then one of the grownups called from the bus door, "Hurry up, everybody! Get a move on!" Naturally, Jeremy tried to run.

That was his third mistake.

It took a while to dig Jeremy out of the mountain of debris of sweaters and Sharon's clothing. As the two sorted out their possessions, Jeremy realized his left arm really hurt. By the end of the day, his elbow had swollen; he spent the weekend with his arm in a sling while everyone else went skiing. He hadn't needed all those sweaters after all.

That was last year. This year Jeremy plans on traveling light—and carrying the bare minimum of baggage. You never know when you'll suddenly have to sprint.

JAILHOUSE OLYMPICS

Today's Bible verse is one of my absolute favorites; I think about it time after time. Paul the Apostle wrote these words, and I think Jeremy would nod his head energetically if he were here to read them with us.

Paul says it's good to travel light, particularly when you're running toward the things that God wants for you. He's already told us that nothing in life can compare with how great it is to know Christ (verse 8). As a matter of fact, he says that anything else is like "garbage" in comparison. So he's in a big hurry to get where God has pointed him—too big a hurry to carry extra baggage, such as worries about the past. He puts all that behind him and strains forward with his eyes on the prize.

Whenever I read that verse, I can see Paul in my mind: straining forward, reaching his hands out, trying to grab God's will for him. Now, would you like to hear the punch line? He wrote those verses from a prison cell. The Romans had locked him up for preaching the gospel. So does the prisoner complain about his cell? Does he make excuses about how it's not possible to serve God behind bars?

Not at all. Paul is filled with infectious, abundant happiness over all the fruit God is *still* producing through him, even from that tiny cell. He's still straining forward like an Olympic sprinter, still striving for all the good things God has in store for him.

If Paul could bear so much fruit from a jail cell, how much could you and I produce? If he could put the unhappiness of confinement behind and push even harder for the goal, why couldn't we?

I think you know the answers to those questions.

RUN HARD, RUN HAPPY

A few verses later, Paul said that he could do *all things* through Christ because He gives us strength (Philippians 4:13). Think of that! If we start from our discovery yesterday—that the key is to want what God wants—and we strain forward to take hold of it, we have no limits. We can do all things because God can do all things. He likes doing them through us.

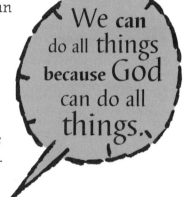

We **can** do all **things because** God can do all **things.**

Yesterday you started to think about wanting what God wants. Today I challenge you to think about the baggage that slows you down. Because, yes, it's one more sneaky way of talking about pruning—our final one. Remember that God does the pruning. If you suddenly see that extra luggage you could stand to leave at home, He is the one helping you see it. God will strengthen you to shed it.

Imagine how it would feel to be light and fast, running toward that goal God has for you. The goal is fruitfulness. The goal is becoming a blessing to everyone you know, and especially to God. You sprint faster and faster, until you feel light, fast, and joyful enough to soar through the clouds. The wind feels good, heaven is closer, you strain forward, and—there—you've grabbed it!

Don't ever let it go.

TALK BACK

When I think of the goals God has for me, here is how I feel:

I'm going to sprint toward that goal this week. One way I'll do it is:

 # WHAT'S THE BIG IDEA?

Have you ever noticed? Olympic sprinters never turn around. They face only one direction.

DAY 22
TAKE IT TO THE NEXT LEVEL

"Abide in Me, and I in you. As the branch cannot bear fruit of itself, unless it abides in the vine, neither can you, unless you abide in Me."

JOHN 15:4 NKJV

READY TO PLAY? Click on the "New Game" icon and prepare for action!

The first level of this video game is the simplest. You move your character through a small maze, searching for the exit. Some of the paths lead to dead ends, but you move on to find the right ones. You're also picking up all kinds of "power boosts" along the way. These are little icons that increase your character's health and power.

Beware of the monsters! They lurk in unexpected places, hoping to pounce on your character and block the way to the next level. You'll need to stop and fight off an attack every now and then. But you keep playing. You keep improving your game. And in time, you get the video screen you've been waiting for: "Congratulations! You've completed the first level." Beneath the words, you see one small green circle: a grape! In this game, we keep score with grapes.

Pretty cool! Wait until you tell your friends how quickly you— But wait! The screen is changing. A new level is beginning. You haven't had time to catch your breath from the last one. Immediately, you see new mazes and new monsters, just a little bit tougher this time. At first you feel frustrated. This is *impossible!* But then you realize those power boosts from the first level give you new abilities.

daY 22

Soon you're making your way through a more difficult level. You get to the exit of level two with two new grape icons to add to the one from last time.

Every day you play a little bit more of the game, and can you believe it? Level twenty-five! Looking back, those first levels seem like kids' stuff. Now you earn whole *clusters* of grapes whenever you make it through a level. The game never ends—it only gets better, deeper, more exciting, and more satisfying. And there's no limit to how many grapes you, the champion, can produce.

GET IN THE GAME

Your life as Jesus' friend and helper is a lot like that video game. It moves from level to level, and the game becomes more complex as you move on. But it also becomes more fruitful and more rewarding. You'll find you can't stop with just a level or two. Instead, you'll be eager to see what your new level in life holds. You can't wait to take on new challenges, gaining the victory over new "monsters," and bearing newer and greater clusters of fruit.

God **wants** you to bear fruit, and to **bear** plenty of it.

The best video games are limited, but God's game never reaches an end as long as you're on this earth. It just keeps getting better and more interesting.

Think about how much we've learned in our first three weeks. By now you take it for granted that God wants you to bear fruit, and to bear plenty of it. You know that we have to grow in order to bear that fruit and that growth requires discipline to keep us pointed in the right direction. You've discovered the secret of pruning, so you know that God will continue to trim away the things that limit your fruit-bearing. There's one more secret: *If you bear lots of fruit, God will invite you to know Him even better. And that will bring the greatest fruit of all.*

Or, to put it in gaming terms: Game Masters keep taking it to the next level until they come to know the Game Designer Himself—and He teaches them the ultimate secrets of the game.

FUTURE FOCUS

As you and I come to our final week together, we reach the far side of the vineyard. We look back across all these wonderful places we've been, and we discover something. We realize that all these big ideas have only made up level one of the adventure. The secrets you've learned here will be a part of your life from now on. You'll move deeper and deeper into the fruit-bearing life He wants for you. Aren't you excited about finding out what lies at the deeper levels of God's challenge for you?

As you bear more fruit, an incredible dream will come true. You'll find God throwing open the doors and inviting you into an even stronger friendship with Him. You'll know and experience Him in a way you never thought possible. And just from spending time with Him, you'll grow wiser, more loving, and more capable of bearing the greatest fruit yet. By that time, your main focus in life will be to do more for God, because you'll understand that it's what your life is all about. The one way you can be completely and totally satisfied is to know Him deeply and to serve Him fully. Everything else is, well, just a game.

These next few days together will be our best yet. As you focus on serving God more fruitfully and knowing God more deeply, well, you can't help but get pumped! Aren't you glad God chose to reveal the secret to you? Aren't you excited about telling others?

TALK BACK

Wow, I've never thought of my faith in God as being like a game!
But here are some ways in which that could be true:

Here is how I feel about taking my relationship with Him to the
next level:

WHAT'S THE BIG IDEA?

*Why stop at the beginner levels? When you serve
God, the best is always in front of you.*

Day 23
Up Close and Personal

But let him who glories glory in this,
That he understands and knows Me.

Jeremiah 9:24 nkjv

Mr. Gonzalez lived right next door all Jamie's life—and Jamie never got to know him until moving day.

Jamie's dad got a new job, and his family was relocating across the country. It was tough to leave the only house he'd ever lived in, but Jamie felt excited about living in a new city. With the rest of his family, he got caught up in all the packing and preparing. What a lot of work that took! They had many things that weren't worth the trouble of packing. Jamie's mom would ask, "Do we really need this picture?" Or, "Why bother to pack up this old exercise bike? Nobody uses it."

Yet there were a few things that were tough to simply throw away. "This is a perfectly good ice cream freezer," Mom said. "We just got a better one. Jamie, run next door and see if Mr. Gonzalez can use it."

Jamie wasn't too thrilled about that suggestion. He'd only seen Mr. Gonzalez out mowing his lawn; they'd never really spoken to each other. But Mom insisted, so Jamie rang the doorbell and asked Mr. Gonzalez if he could use an ice cream freezer. "Come in," the neighbor said with a smile. "I have someone on the phone, but I'll be right with you."

Jamie had a surprise coming. As he waited in the living room, he saw baseball pictures all over the walls. There were plaques made of balls and bats—pictures of Mr. Gonzalez with the biggest stars in the game. It took about thirty seconds for Jamie to realize that Mr. Gonzalez was none other than Felipe Gonzalez, the retired All-Star third baseman. Suddenly, Jamie was much more interested in talking to his neighbor.

He left with an autographed ball and a handshake. That was nice, but as he moved far across the country, Jamie couldn't help but think about the friendship he could have enjoyed with the major league star next door.

SO NEAR, YET SO FAR

Don't you feel a little sorry for Jamie? All during the trip to his new home he kept thinking, *It could have been so cool, so awesome. But how did I know?*

The good news is that your story can have a much happier ending. Today's Bible verse says that when it comes to famous friends, you can have the ultimate bragging rights. I talk to many people who tell me, "I never realized God was so close all this time. I never knew about the friendship that could have been mine, the relationship that I could have just reached out and claimed any day. I never knew God was so available to me."

> When you say "yes" to Jesus, His **Spirit** comes to live right there within **you.**

You see, we could say that God is everyone's next-door neighbor—but it's actually closer than that. When you say "yes" to Jesus, His Spirit comes to live right there within you. You don't have to go knock on any doors to talk to Him. Wherever you go, even if you travel a thousand miles away, He's right there with you. No space-ship could ever take you out of range of His voice.

Sadly, many people never realize this. They go through life without that close friendship. Don't you dare be one of those people! You can do a lot better than walk away with the handshake and an autographed picture. You can know what it's like to be among God's very closest and dearest friends. It's the best relationship you'll ever experience.

TAKE THE TEST

As I've thought about our friendship with God, I've come up with five levels of closeness. Read each of these and think about which one best describes your relationship with God. You might want to put a check mark next to it.

___ *Aloof.* God seems far away, like someone in another city. He's not a part of my everyday life and interests.

___ *Acquaintance.* God is like someone in another class at school—someone I speak to occasionally, but not often.

___ *Associate.* God is like someone in my class, not my closest friend but someone who is a part of my everyday life.

___ *Affectionate.* God is becoming a very close friend. He's someone I really enjoy, and someone I want to know even better.

___ *Abiding.* God is my very best, very closest friend. Being with Him is the best thing there is in life. More and more, His goals and interests are becoming my own.

If you think about it, everybody fits into one of those five categories—and everybody has the opportunity to move into a different one. Today's idea is that you can always take the next step. You can come to know God in a deeper way than you do today. I hope you'll think this week about how you can take one step closer. The best friend imaginable is so close. Why not reach out?

daY 23

TALK BACK

Here is the A-word that I checked on page 91, and here's why I would use it to describe my relationship with God:

Here are a couple of ways I might move to a new level in my friend-ship with God:

⭐ WHAT'S THE BIG IDEA?

In friendship with God, every day is moving day—but make sure you're moving in the right direction.

Day 24
GET BUSY ABIDING

*God is love, and he who abides in love abides in God,
and God in him.*

1 JOHN 4:16 NKJV

HAVE YOU EVER KNOWN SIBLINGS who seemed to have come from different planets? It happens—maybe it's true in your family.

Mary and Martha were a little like that. Guests were coming, and the two sisters reacted in completely different ways. They expected a full house, including their friend Jesus and all the disciples. Mary and Martha were two of Jesus' closest friends, and they were excited about entertaining Him in their home.

Whenever I think of those two, the one I can most easily picture is Martha. Have you ever known a Martha? She was a nervous wreck, running in and out of rooms, balancing nine plates and seven cups, hanging up cloaks—taking care of everything and everyone. I can just see her almost tripping over her sister, who quietly sat at Jesus' feet. And I can see the smoke coming out of her ears! Here she was working *so* hard to care for her guests, and there was her sister sitting around, taking it easy. Did you know that Martha actually tattled to Jesus? It's in Luke 10:40. Martha said, in so many words, "Jesus, I'm breaking my back here, all by myself! Can you tell my lazy sister to pull her share of the load?"

To which Jesus only smiled and said, "Martha, Martha, you are worried and troubled about many things. But one thing is needed, and Mary has chosen that good part, which will not be taken away from her" (Luke 10:41–42 NKJV).

We're not told how Martha took that reply, but don't you think she must have been shocked? She'd been taught the same thing as you and I: to work and keep busy. Even going to God's house, the church, is all about busyness and activities, isn't it? But Jesus said, "Only one thing is important." Surely not laziness! What do you think He meant?

It's About Abiding

Let's be clear on one thing: Jesus didn't teach us to spend our time sitting and watching others work. I don't want to hear that you used today's reading to get out of cleaning your room!

Jesus did make this point: The wonderful opportunity to know Him deeply tends to get lost in all our commotion and running around. We simply like busyness and accomplishment. Your life and

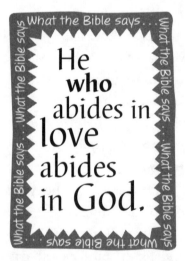

He **who** abides in love abides in God.

mine are more like the chaos of Christmas morning gift-opening with the family than the quietness of Christmas morning in a Bethlehem stable.

But we need some quiet time to know God, don't we? We need to shut down all the busyness and spend some time simply *being* with God. We call that abiding, and it's at the very heart of the secrets of the vine. Sadly, too many Christians I meet don't even know how to simply abide. But if you want to know God deeply, and you want to bear fruit abundantly, it begins with abiding in His presence. All that means is doing what Mary did: sitting at the feet of Jesus, giving all our loving attention to what He has to say to us.

It's not so easy at first, is it? At least Mary had Jesus right there in the flesh, speaking real words she could hear. But actually, we have Jesus in a much deeper, much more powerful way. Can that be possible? Yes, through His Spirit living within us. As your life goes on, you'll learn how to abide more and more with Jesus, and to hear His words just as Martha did.

LAWS OF LISTENING

I imagine I have your full attention now. Most people are very interested in knowing exactly how they can experience God. Let's list a few key points about listening to God.

Abide with the Person, not the program. Reading your Bible is important, but it's not the same as abiding. Going to church is a must, but it's not the same as abiding. There isn't a program or a procedure. You simply seek God Himself, and ask Him to abide with you.

Abiding is available to anyone, anywhere, at any time. That's the great thing. This isn't an exclusive club; anyone who wants to know God has that privilege. And you can abide with God anywhere, from a loud school cafeteria to your vacation at the beach.

Abiding has no limits. Someone said we're like glasses of water that keep growing in size as we're filled; we can never be full because we keep developing new capacity. There's always more of God to know.

Abiding takes effort. It won't happen by itself. You must keep pursuing God, staying deeply committed to your desire to know Him.

Well, that's enough to get you started. It may be a little uncomfortable at first, like getting to know a new cousin you've never met. But keep at it! Talk to God. Tell Him how much you want not just to know Him but also to abide with Him. Do you think He'll ignore such a request? Not a chance!

daY 24

TALK BACK

If I had to draw a scale with Mary at one end (abiding) and Martha at the other (acting), here is where I would place myself, and why:

Here is how I think I could try spending some time with God:

WHAT'S THE BIG IDEA?

Meaning business with God doesn't always mean busyness for God.

DAY 25
WAITING? FOR ME?

"As the Father loved Me, I also have loved you; abide in My love."

JOHN 15:9 NKJV

IF THEY GAVE OUT TROPHIES for bad days, Liz would have just earned a colossal one. She set a new career record for worst day. After today, she'll probably be inducted into the Bad Day Hall of Fame. If days were doughnuts, they would have scraped Liz's into the garbage disposal. Well, you get the idea.

After the lecture by Mom, which came after getting pushed around on the school bus, which came after the tear-filled argument with her best friend, which came after the D on the history test, which came after the mystery meat at lunch, Liz stormed into her room and slammed the door. She threw herself down on her bed, pounded both fists into the mattress, and said, "Aaarrrrggghhh! GRRRRRRRR!" She *almost* said a bad word. But at that very moment she heard the polite cough.

Liz looked up and saw the angel, sitting at the desk. Liz said— nothing. All she could do was stare. He was definitely an angel. He was wonderful, bigger than life, shining with the glory of God, and more beautiful than anyone or anything on earth. He only smiled calmly in her direction, and his smile was like a rainbow.

Finally, Liz mustered the courage to ask, in a trembling voice, "Why are you here?"

The angel said, "I'm waiting for my appointment with God. It's right after yours."

day 25

Liz said, "But why here? Why would you have to wait behind me? I'm such a mess, and I'm afraid I forget my appointments with God all the time."

"Sure, but God waits for you here anyway, every single day," said the angel. "You're tops on His list, Priority One. I have to wait my turn, and I always know I can find Him here because He loves being with you."

Liz's day just got much better.

HARD TO IMAGINE

Now, why would I tell you such a wild story? It's true that I made it up, but the basic point isn't made up at all. If God had to choose between you and the greatest of His angels, you would win every time. Have you ever thought about that? You would win in a heart-

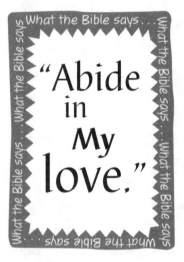

"Abide in My love."

beat, because you *are* God's heartbeat. As His child, you're His deepest joy. Our verse today tells us that we are loved with the kind of love that goes on between the Father and Jesus, His Son. He loves you enough to wait every day, from now until forever, hoping you'll look His way.

I make such a big point out of this because you and I struggle to even take in how much God loves us. We have no trouble understanding His anger, His discipline, or His perfection and holi-

ness. But His love? Perfect love is something we can't begin to understand. So we're a little blurry when it comes to His incredible love for us. If you had written the story I shared, perhaps it would have been different. Perhaps the angel would have scowled and said, "Aren't you ashamed of yourself—worrying about all those trivial things that God doesn't even care about. He's going to give you one more chance, so you'd better shape up!"

You can see the guilt and the shame there. But that's not how God calls to us—not in the least. He never says, "Hurry up! I'm going to give you *such* a lecture!" Instead He gently whispers, "Come on, let's go to your room, where you can get comfortable. Let's spend some time together, just you and Me. You can tell Me about all the things on your mind because I love to hear about them. I can tell you all the wonderful plans I have for you. And if you like, we can just sit quietly and enjoy each other's company."

That's the kind of love I'm talking about.

GETTING BETTER ALL THE TIME

Abide is another word for "remain"; "stay awhile"; "hang out." Where do you enjoy hanging out the most? Maybe at a friend's home. Maybe at the mall. Maybe with an uncle, an aunt, or your grand-parents. Different places make good "hangouts" for different reasons.

God wants you to come to a time when constantly, everywhere you go, you're hanging out with Him. While playing a game of kickball, you might realize that He is right there with you. *I'm glad You're here,* you'll think. *Help me not to lose my temper, and help me be a good friend.* Or you might stop in the middle of a math test and think, *Lord, it's good to know You're with me during this test. Help me focus. Thank You for being here.* It doesn't matter to God where you are; He just enjoys your abiding with Him.

As you get better and better at that, the time will come when you won't be able to bear the thought of not being with God, which is okay, because that's impossible anyway. He's the Friend who *never* deserts you, no matter what, even when you've set a new career record for bad days.

That's the kind of love I'm talking about.

TALK BACK

God is always waiting patiently to be with me. Here's how that makes me feel:

I guess it's so hard for me to imagine how much God loves me because:

WHAT'S THE BIG IDEA?

You're at the top of God's "To Do" list every day. If He had a wallet, your picture would be in front.

Day 26
Devotional Database

As the deer pants for the water brooks,
So pants my soul for You, O God.
My soul thirsts for God, for the living God.
When shall I come and appear before God?

Psalm 42:1–2 nkjv

Imagine you receive an invitation in the mail. It's a very special invitation. You're invited to become a beta-tester for some new computer software, direct from heaven.

A beta-tester, you realize, is someone who helps test-run a new computer program before it's released to the rest of the world. That's cool! But heavenly software? It turns out (at least in this unlikely story) that your computer can be hooked up to heaven's database through a special modem. You can get all kinds of cool spiritual information.

So you install the software. Now you can click on that new icon and, just like that, you're hooked up to heaven. Where do you begin? Check the log on your sins from yesterday? No fun there. Surf through the new halo designs? No thanks. Maybe you should ask a really tough question. That's it! So you type in, "What is the secret of life?" Boy, this is gonna be good! You'd better load up the printer—the answer might be longer than your math textbook!

After you click the "Send" button, your screen says, "Please wait." Is that the secret of life? No, just an instruction—you wait for the question to be processed. Finally, it comes up on the screen.

Here is what it says:

- *Read the Bible daily.*
- *Pray constantly.*
- *Share your faith regularly.*

You stare at the screen. That's *it*? You have heavenly data access, and that's the best it can do? Surely it's a bug in the program! You type in another question: "How can I find God?" You wait—and again you get a three-point response. *And it's the same three points!*

Is the software malfunctioning—or could the answers be so simple?

It's Not Rocket Science

Sometimes we make things too hard. Have you ever done that, say, with a new math concept in school? I know a lot of people who do it with their daily devotions (their time for abiding with God).

There isn't any complex, complicated formula for spending time getting to know God. But there are really good guidelines you can remember. Let's go over a few:

Be organized about it. A baseball or basketball team doesn't just practice whenever team members feel like it; they set a time and they keep to it. You should set a daily time for spending focused time with God, and be devoted to it. Morning works best for many people, but choose the time when you're most comfortable with God and not in a hurry.

Read your Bible. Start with a psalm or perhaps Phillipians, James, or one of Paul's letters. If possible, use a guide published for someone your age. You might ask a parent or a church leader to help you find one. Work through the guide or one section of the Bible, picking up where you left off the day before. Read just a few verses, enough to think about.

Pray. Talk to God, using your own words. Feel free to talk about the things you're interested in. God cares about them because you do. Just relax and talk to Him as you would anyone else.

Keep a diary about your friendship with God. Write out your new ideas from Bible study and keep track of the things you ask God to do. Then you can keep a record of how He answers your prayers.

THE ABSOLUTE, ULTIMATE, NUMERO UNO, BOTTOM-LINE SECRET OF ABIDING

I'm going to give you one more secret to keep in mind as you seek God every day. This is the big one, because there is a sad truth you need to know: It's possible to do all the things I listed above *without* ever abiding with God. All those things are good tools to help you, but they're not the same as actually experiencing the presence of God. That happens when your heart gets involved, and you really want to know God. Here is our final point:

Pursue God with all your heart. Make yourself a promise that you will keep seeking Him until you've found Him. This is a discipline to hold for the rest of your life. For right now, it will take some concentration—and patience—to really begin to know what abiding with God is all about. Remember, He has promised to be available to you. "And you will seek Me and find Me, when you search for Me with all your heart" (Jeremiah 29:13 NKJV).

But be patient. Don't let yourself become discouraged or frustrated. Never give up chasing after God. The time will come when it will happen: You'll realize that He's with you *and you can feel it.* You'll be overjoyed, and you'll never want to let go.

The "secrets" of abiding with God couldn't be simpler. You've heard them before, and you'll hear them again. But the real secret, the one that makes the difference, is what we've discussed. *Keep on keeping on.* Pursue God—after all, He's always pursuing you.

TALK BACK

To me, the most exciting thing about pursuing God is:

I suppose the reason that it takes such patience to seek God is:

WHAT'S THE BIG IDEA?

*Pursue God with determination, never forgetting
that He loves it when you catch Him.*

Day 27
Hope for the Hyped

The LORD is near to all who call upon Him,
To all who call upon Him in truth.

PSALM 145:18 NKJV

ANDRÉ JUST FINISHED THE KOOL KIDS KAMP-OUT with his church group, and he is supremely pumped. Awesomely energized. Atomically charged. I'd go so far as to say he's galvanized, and I haven't said *that* about anybody else in this book.

André came, he saw, he bought the T-shirt. But he also heard three different Christian bands and two cool speakers, both of whom got in his face and challenged him to get into God's Word and *stay* there, dude. Pitch a tent. Lay down some roots. All the kids got hyped. At the end of the weekend, they took a pledge, right out loud, to hang onto God's Word so tightly that *nothing or nobody* could scrape them off! They all pumped their fists, gave high-fives, and awesomely energized each other.

But Matthew isn't buying it. Matthew is André's number-one pal, a kid who tends to roll his eyes a lot. He didn't go to the Kool Kids Kamp-Out. He says, "André, you were awesomely energized at *last* year's Kool Kids Kamp-Out. You were awesomely energized at the Righteous Regiment Revival Rally, and you were awesomely energized at the Wild, Wild Weekend o'Worship. Matter of fact, I'm not even gonna mention how supremely pumped you were about the new X-Infinity skateboard, which you were going to devote your life to mastering. Isn't it packed away somewhere in your basement?"

Boy, that last remark was a cheap shot. Matthew has a way of letting the air out of a kid's balloon, and it's annoying. André has decided to find other friends to hang out with. But he has this nagging feeling: What if Matthew is right? André made a commitment to dig into God's Word, but what if it comes to no more than last summer's skateboard fad? His last attempt at spending daily time with God lasted three days. Is that as good as it gets?

JUST DO IT!

I'd love to tell André to hold his chin up. This is a problem most of us have, and I bet you've had it, too. We get so excited about spending time with God—or about some new game, possession, or almost anything else—that we set our hopes sky-high. It feels good to be

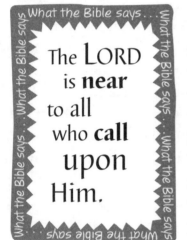

The LORD is **near** to all who **call** upon Him.

excited about something, and it seems as if these are *forever* feelings. But feelings are never forever; they come and they go.

Just to make my point, I'll predict that André will forgive Matthew—at least I hope he will, because Matthew needs to be around some Christian friends. Right now, André is angry with him. But that, too, is only a feeling, and it's likely to pass.

If feelings are so unpredictable and unreliable, perhaps we should use something else as the basis for our friendship with God. Do you get the point? While I'm all hyped up about spending time with Jesus today, I might not have that emotion tomorrow. So instead of spending time with Jesus as the response to some emotion, I'll spend time with Jesus for another reason. I'll do so because I've made a commitment to, because He has commanded me to, and because I know in my mind I'm going to be much happier if I do.

This morning I climbed out of bed and brushed my teeth. Guess what? I wasn't awesomely energized about brushing my teeth. I just did it because it was the right thing to do. I didn't even have to think about it because it's become a habit—a part of me. Now let me be clear: Meeting with God is a whole lot more exciting than brushing my teeth. But even when my feelings aren't there, my will to meet with Him is. Meeting every single day with God is a part of me, and abiding with Him is who I am.

And when I stop to think about *that*—I get supremely pumped!

NAILING IT DOWN

Don't coast on your feelings when it comes to abiding with God. Feelings run out of momentum, like André's enthusiasm for his skateboard—then comes the crash. Base your plans instead on *commitment*. That's a way of saying, "This is something important to me—a lot more important than taking a shower or brushing my teeth. I can do this, and I can keep doing it. So I will. I may run hot and cold emotionally, but God is constant. He wants to meet with me every day, so I'm going to nail it down right now. I'm making the decision to abide with God on a daily basis, whether I feel excited or not."

Remember yesterday? We talked about setting a time and making an appointment. If you waited until you felt like going to see the dentist, you'd never go—that's what appointments are for. Set your daily time, stick to it, and don't worry. The feelings will follow.

That's what André is going to do, and he's awesomely . . . well, never mind. It makes no difference in the long run whether he's awesomely energized or heavily hyped. What counts is that he's confidently committed.

daY 27

TALK BACK

The best time for me to meet daily with God is:

The most effective way for me not to run out of steam is to:

WHAT'S THE BIG IDEA?

Feelings are like snow—pretty, but they make lousy build-ing materials. Commitment is like rock. Rock on!

DAY 28
ROCK SOLID

*Know the love of Christ which passes knowledge; that you may be filled
with all the fullness of God. Now to Him who is able to do exceedingly
abundantly above all that we ask or think, according to the
power that works in us.*

EPHESIANS 3:19–20 NKJV

ONCE UPON A TIME THERE was a little village with a wonderful
leader. He loved the people and they loved him. When he died, the
people wondered how to replace him. They decided to hold the
position open until they could find a man who resembled their
great leader in every way. They sculpted his profile into the side of
a cliff overlooking the city, just so they'd all remember his face.

Meanwhile, the village council kept searching for a worthy
successor. They traveled abroad, always looking for features to
match the ones on the cliff. Back home, there was a young man
who listened eagerly for news of their search. He lived in a little
cottage at the base of the cliff, and every day he gazed at the great
face above him. As he plowed the fields and cut his wood, his eyes
scanned that face, reflecting on the greatness of every feature. In
time, there wasn't a curve or a line in those massive features that
he didn't know by heart. All his thoughts were directed to the
goodness of the leader from long ago.

After years of searching, the council gave up. Try though they
might, they could find no face to match the one in the rocks, so
they headed home. Upon entering the city, they stopped to rest at

the young man's cottage at the foot of the cliff. As he came out to meet them, he saw their faces turn pale and their jaws drop in surprise. Can you guess why?

Yes, you're a step ahead of me. The young man had become a perfect replica of the past ruler. Not only did he look the part, but he also shared that level of wisdom and goodness. Over time, he had become what he most loved and studied.

CARVED UPON YOUR HEART

Nathaniel Hawthorne wrote "The Great Stone Face," and I think you know where I'm going with that story. Jesus said that where our treasures are, our hearts will follow. What is a treasure? It's the thing you love most. And what is your heart? Jesus meant the truest reflection of your identity. You become what you love and admire.

Think of the face of Jesus looking over your life, so that every day you study it closely. Every day you reflect at school and at home on His wisdom and love. As you watch television, you think, "What does Jesus think about this?" When you see a friend who needs help, you think, "What would Jesus do?"

Of course, the face of Jesus isn't made of lifeless stone. Its features are etched not in the rock but in your heart. You can know Him by abiding with Him—the thing we've talked about all week. His wisdom can become your wisdom. His thoughts and desires can become your own. Wouldn't you like that? The time will come when your friends and family will look upon you and be shocked—you'll be the very image of Jesus, etched in flesh and blood.

The Bible says that God has known you since He laid out the blueprint for this world. And He has planned for you to conform more each day to the pattern of Jesus: "For whom He foreknew, He also predestined to be conformed to the image of His Son, that He might be the firstborn among many brethren" (Romans 8:29 NKJV).

Sounds exciting, doesn't it? Each day you'll be a little more like Jesus in your words and your actions.

OVER THE TOP

Read today's Bible passage (Ephesians 3:19–20) very closely. It says that the love of Christ is greater than you can ever take in, no matter how hard you try. It's like staring at the sculpted features every day and always seeing something new. And when God's power fills us up, He begins working in us to do "exceedingly abundantly above all that we ask or think" (Ephesians 3:20 NKJV).

How much? Above all you could ask or think. How much above? *Abundantly* above. How abundantly above? *Exceedingly* abundantly above. Paul, who wrote those words, nailed on every descriptive word he could to make triple-sure that you didn't miss the point. God wants to do way, way more for you than you could ever ask or imagine. *Over-the-top* more. *Mega*-more.

As you read your Bible every day, as you spend time with God, as you abide in His presence, that's what will happen to you. He'll fill you with these things: love, confidence, power, ser-

> God wants to do way, way more for you than you could ever ask or imagine.

vanthood, and wisdom. And He'll use you every single day in some exciting new way. One day you'll exclaim, "I can't believe what God is doing through me. It's so much more than I could ever have asked. It's far beyond anything I could have even *imagined*."

That's what He's done in my life, and I want so much for it to happen for you. It will, if you simply abide with Him. Count on it; it's written in stone.

TALK BACK

Here's what I learned from the story of "The Great Stone Face":

Here are the ways I think I will change as I abide with God:

WHAT'S THE BIG IDEA?

*Jesus is the Rock of Ages, and you can
be a chip off the old block!*

Day 29
Bright New Wings

See how the farmer waits for the precious fruit of the earth, waiting patiently for it until it receives the early and latter rain. You also be patient. Establish your hearts.

James 5:7–8 NKJV

CHAN WANDERED THROUGH THE WOODS last spring. That's her favorite time of year. Everything about it seems beautiful and special. Chan likes the colors that pop up in the most surprising places. She likes the lovely music of the birds. She loves the way the whole earth seems to shake off winter and come back to life, and she even likes the smell of newness. Chan was made for springtime.

So there she was, rambling aimlessly with a big smile on her face. Then something caught her eye—and she caught her breath. There, hanging from the limb of a tree, a little bundle swung back and forth, trembling. Chan recognized it immediately as a cocoon, and she knew what was happening: Her favorite little creature, the homely caterpillar, had become a gorgeous butterfly and was making its way into the world.

Chan loves the whole story of the butterfly, because it tells her that beautiful things come from surprising packages. She was breathless with excitement about the opportunity to see the miracle happen before her own eyes—a butterfly sharing its beauty with the world for the first time.

Chan had no idea how many minutes passed as she watched the tiny, unfolding miracle. But it worried her: Why wasn't the butterfly making better progress? The little creature didn't seem to have the strength to break through the cocoon.

Chan wanted that first glimpse of bright, new wings beating against the air. She couldn't bear the thought of a butterfly struggling like that. So she decided to help the poor creature. Taking a nail file from her pocket, she gently cut into the cocoon to make the creature's work a bit easier.

HURRY UP AND WAIT!

You probably know already that Chan made a mistake. God has been making caterpillars and butterflies for a long time now, and He gave them a perfect system for flight training. In the process of fighting through the webbing of the cocoon, the caterpillar builds important muscles and becomes what God intended. The struggles are a part of God's plan: They force the little butterfly to build up the muscles it will need for flying.

> The **really** important things in life take patience.

But as Chan sadly discovered, there are no shortcuts. To hurry the insect before its time is to leave it with an unprepared body—one never likely to fly.

Chan felt badly about her mistake, but now she respects God's creation even more deeply. She understands just how beautifully and thoughtfully He designed our world—even the parts that involve pain and struggling. Here's a hard lesson for all of us—you can't imagine how hard it is for me. The really important things in life take patience. That includes bearing fruit for God. There is some fruit you can bear today, and some that won't be ready for many years. I'm told that the best grape-growing regions often take fifty years to produce their finest fruit.

I can imagine that you're excited about the ideas we've discussed over the last month. I know you'd like to go right to the head of the class in serving God. You'd like to see some of that fabulous fruit immediately.

My advice is to hurry up—and wait. What do I mean by that? You can start your wonderful life as a branch of the vine right now—so hurry up; do it! But you must also wait for the very best fruit that God will bear through you. So wait; be patient!

You'll Love the Wings!

Chan learned a big lesson through her episode with the cocoon. The struggle in life is important. We can't simply throw it away or take a shortcut, because God uses it to make us wiser and stronger. There will be discipline in your life, and that's a course correction any budding butterfly should understand. There will be pruning, and any caterpillar knows about cutting away everything that would keep you from flying. All the while, you can be abiding. That's what makes it all worthwhile. God whispers into your ear, "For now, you're a caterpillar. But you're going to love the wings I have for you."

Do you feel like a "cater-fly" today—a little clumsy and green, but ready to take flight in Technicolor? Hurry up and wait. As we agreed earlier, the best is always yet to come for God's creatures—whether you're a branch or the caterpillar creeping upon it.

daY 29

TALK BACK

Sometimes I feel like a "cater-fly" because:

Here are some good things to hurry on, and here are some things that will take waiting:

  WHAT'S THE BIG IDEA?

Every caterpillar is a butterfly in training.
Get ready for takeoff!

Day 30
The Winning Team

And let us consider one another in order to stir up love and good works, not forsaking the assembling of ourselves together, as is the manner of some, but exhorting one another, and so much the more as you see the Day approaching.

Hebrews 10:24–25 NKJV

WHEN CALEB DISCOVERED HIKING, he became a changed person. Some people just like to walk, and that's Caleb—but he also likes all the stuff that goes along with it. He likes the feeling of making it all the way up a steep climb, and he likes recognizing the kinds of trees and plants.

Caleb was very excited to find a group of other kids (and a couple of adults) who shared his love of walking in the wilderness. They made plans to take a different trek every weekend they could, often camping out on Saturday nights in order to finish the hike on Sunday. Campfire chats and ration-sharing tend to build friendships, and Caleb became very close to the others in his group. But one issue gnawed at him.

Caleb had always gone to church with his parents. But now he was becoming more mature in his faith as he learned about the Bible and about living as a believer. Sunday mornings meant worship and Bible study with kids his age—until he became camping-crazy. His parents mentioned that he hiked so often these days that he missed a lot of church. They were concerned.

When they brought up the subject, Caleb's first reaction was,

"But I like camping!" But he also had to admit they were right. He had missed most of a unit on John's gospel in his Bible study group. Caleb felt caught in the middle. What should he do?

He talked to Mr. Antonio, one of the adults in the hiking group, who immediately understood. He said, "Caleb, your church activities are important. What if you joined us for some Saturday hikes, and we got you back in time for church on Sundays?" Caleb's face lit up.

He's still hiking, but his Christian walk comes before his walk in the woods.

COME TOGETHER

Today's verses, taken from Hebrews, help us remember that being a Christian involves *togetherness*. I talk to many people who struggle with their faith all alone. Not only is that unnecessary, but it's also a violation of what the Bible commands us to do.

> The church isn't brick and mortar at all—it's flesh and blood.

Notice how our passage puts it: Think about others; help others. That's what the church is all about. When we say the word *church*, most people think of a building. But the church isn't brick and mortar at all—it's flesh and blood. It's people realizing that when we come together, we add up to a power greater than the sum of our parts. The best way to fail in your mission of fruit-bearing is to try to function all by yourself. God designed you to operate in group mode. And here's something exciting: He gave you gifts and talents that stand out as soon as you're plugged in to the local church.

All the things we've talked about—fruit-bearing, discipline, pruning, abiding—are enhanced and improved by your relationships in the body of Christ, which is exactly what the Bible tells us the church is. Your friends will think about you and help you; you'll do the same for them. Bonding together makes all of us strong. That's why you should walk together, down the winding trail that leads toward lovely, abundant fruit in your life.

I'm like Caleb; I like to hike. The woods are nice, but there's no better journey than the one I take with my Savior walking before me and my friends walking beside me. On that hike, you and I will never walk alone.

daY 30

TALK BACK

I know that church is important, and here's my favorite thing about it:

Here are some ways I can plug in better at my church:

WHAT'S THE BIG IDEA?

When you plug into the church, the power flows and the light shines.

DAY 31
FRUIT, FACES, AND FUTURE

"This is my command: Love each other as I have loved you.
The greatest love a person can show is to die for his friends."
JOHN 15:12–13 ICB

AND SO WE COME TO THE END, which really means the beginning. Let's see if I can explain that for you.

I hope you've enjoyed this past month as much as I have. We've sat quietly in the corner of the upper room where Jesus spoke with His friends over dinner. We've heard Him reveal four incredible secrets of the vine. And we have taken a close look at each one. Here we are on our thirty-first day together, but we know that things can't be the same now. This may be the end of a little book, but it's the beginning of a new life for you.

I hope you'll keep the image of lovely, abundant grapes in your mind. I hope that if I happen to see you five years from now, you'll be able to tell me what the secrets are—and how you've seen them in action in your life. I hope you'll have a big smile on your face, because you'll know you're on your way to producing unbelievable fruit for God. And perhaps I can speak to some of that fruit.

What? Another odd statement! Allow me to explain myself once again.

After we've looked at the fruit long enough, we no longer see grapes, for that's just the word-picture to help us understand. What we see are *faces*. These are the faces of people you've helped to know God. They're people who have begun to bear their own fruit. And that starts an incredible chain reaction. It's like grape seeds being scattered by the wind. Soon there's beautiful fruit growing everywhere—enough to feed the world.

You'll see some of your fruitfulness, and it will make you very, very happy. But you'll never see the full extent of it. You'll never know just how widely God used you—until you meet Him face to face.

A Window into the Future

Remember that angel from a few days back? Let's say you and the angel struck up a friendship (angels are handy friends to have!).

One day you're sitting in your room when you ask him to do something really cool for you. You'd like to see it all. You'd like to know just how far your fruitfulness stretched. So the angel says, "Think I can do that for you—just this once. Afterward, of course, I'll have to wipe it out of your memory."

You ask why he'll have to do that, and he replies, "Because you would be overwhelmed. Seeing your own eternal impact would be more than you could handle." Then the angel asks you to look out the window. All you can see is a great sea of faces, stretching out for miles and miles. It's an entire human landscape extending from your window. And the only ones you recognize are those on the first row! How can this be?

> What the Bible says . . .
>
> "Love each other as I have loved you."

The angel anticipates your question. He says, "You touch a great number of people around you—your family and close friends, for example. But they influence others, too. When God uses you, He reaches right through you to touch the next circle, then the one beyond that, and on and on. In time, the seeds from your fruit will lead to clusters that can only be counted in heaven."

You have to sit down on the bed to take that in. Could you bear that much fruit? You must start where you are; it all begins at your window. Jesus is the true vine, the only vine, and it's time to branch out toward a fruitful future. And someday, perhaps you and I will see each other in heaven, where we can count the faces. For now, we've got work to do!

daY 31

TALK BACK

I know God wants to use me in the lives of people, including:

When I think of how awesome my influence may someday be, it makes me realize that:

WHAT'S THE BIG IDEA?

Fruit, faces, future, forever—it's not so far from this moment to heaven. May God bear beautiful fruit through your life!